Murder in Mombasa

Robert Gribbin

Published by Robert Gribbin, 2013.

Murder in Mombasa

By Robert E. Gribbin
Published by Robert E. Gribbin at Smashwords
Copyright 2013 Robert E. Gribbin

This is a fictionalized account of a real event. Names have been changed; plot manipulated, dialogue invented and characters created in order to spin the tale.

The Calm

I stood, thighs pressed against the wall looking out my 7th floor window; below stretched a canopy of green leafed trees interspersed by rusted metal and the odd red terracotta tile roofs of English Point. Beyond was the deep blue of the Indian Ocean where riding at anchor a mile or so offshore was the gray behemoth of an aircraft carrier, the USS America. The America was the center piece of a naval battle group of eleven ships that arrived earlier that morning for three days of liberty. This meant 10,000 American sailors would be, in their jargon "hitting the beach" for rest and relaxation. My task as U.S. Consul in Mombasa was to ride herd on this whirlwind, plan and organize as could best be done ahead of time, be involved in the admiral's protocol visits to the Provincial Commissioner, the Kenyan Navy Commander and the Mayor, host a party for the dignitaries and be invited in turn to be a guest aboard. Finally I would have to pick up the pieces afterwards – help collect those left behind and assuage merchants and hoteliers that bills, especially for damages, would be paid. It usually worked out, but one never knew. Ten thousand guys could wreak a lot of havoc, even as they engendered good will and poured a huge amount of money into the economy's coffers.

I remembered that thus far during my two years in Mombasa ship visits had gone well. Yet, a murder that occurred about five years earlier still haunted us in a fashion. An American sailor had owned up to strangling a prostitute in a drunken rage. He stood trial in a Kenyan court and was convicted of a lesser charge of manslaughter, but then released instead of imprisoned. This outcome outraged the public, especially since the presiding judge was British. Charges of racism and of the U.S. buying the verdict abounded.

Money was the attraction for the locals. Much of the coast's economy was based on tourism, and the sailors bought curios and souvenirs, drank, ate, rented hotel rooms, visited nearby game parks, patronized casinos, nightclubs and prostitutes. A few always managed to get in trouble for fighting, drunkenness, dope, or stupidly running afoul of some scam artist. U.S. Navy Shore Patrol officers coordinated with local police to minimize the impact and remove trouble makers quickly. Yet there was an altruistic side to the visit. We organized basketball and soccer games as well as a mini-marathon. There was always a group prepared for a service project of some sort – later that morning I would be meeting a chaplain and a team of about thirty men who would paint several rooms in the old folk's home, Mji wa Salaama, near the causeway. Ships often brought "operation handclasp" material for distribution. Usually this included pallets of primary school books that had been replaced by the state of California, boxes of medical supplies such as bandages and all kinds of hospital one-use kits, plus outdated medicines, a pallet or two of used clothing – once I found enough different red and orange tees shirts from Jack's hamburgers to outfit two soccer teams. Occasionally there was a pallet of sewing equipment even with a trundle machine or one containing soccer balls and basketballs. In any case, I learned through experience that we needed to sort out handclasp material prior to giving it away. Thus, I kept a sorted supply from a previous visit ready to go. Recipients were identified and notified so that the current naval visitors could leave new goods with us for sorting and deliver others that were appropriate to deserving recipients.

It was hot as usual in Mombasa, but not oppressively so. The sea breeze stirred, waiting for the monsoon winds to change. The sense of expectation in the city was high. Among other things, such a massive number of visitors provided great theater, evidence that Mombasa counted in the great scheme of the world. I crossed my fingers in hope that nothing untoward would happen. Of course, I would be proven wrong.

Before leaving the consulate, I looked in for U.S. Navy Senior Chief Petty Officer Karl Woodley, but he had already left on his rounds. He was a crusty career man, whom I had once addressed as "chief" only to be abruptly corrected. "It's senior chief" I was told. Woodley's responsibilities were logistical. He made arrangements with the port authority for berthing, fuel and water. He passed ships' provision requests – lots of fruits and vegetables - on to vendors and ensured delivery. He coordinated cargo or personnel arriving at the airport via USAF flights and arranged for it or them to be transported to the port or lifted by chopper out to the carrier. In short, he was indispensable to a successful port call. For a big visit like the current one, his operation would be beefed up, in particular by several Naval Investigative Service personnel with an anti-drug mandate who would prepare the way for Shore Patrol coordination with local police. AIDS was also becoming a problem and the Navy was sensitive to its presence in Kenya. Thus, warnings about the link between sexual activity and AIDS were prominently conveyed to sailors prior to arrival in port.

I had a full program for the day. Sebastian was waiting at the door, the car ready with the U.S. flag flying.

On Board

Jim Tyrell smelled the sweet tropical breeze that wafted into the hanger deck. It carried the scent of land and of flowers. It pushed back the stink of grease, oil and jet fuel that normally characterized the area. Nearby some of the F-18 Tomcat jets, the offensive strike power of the carrier, were carefully parked, wings folded in an orderly fashion, ready to roll quickly to the massive elevators that would lift them to the flight deck once the carrier was again underway. Planes, however, were not his business and he was rarely even allowed onto the main deck. Jim's job was maintenance of ship systems, a glorified rating for a plumber he often thought. Yet he felt part of this vast war machine. Everything had to mesh in order for the ship to perform, even the toilets.

Jim liked the navy. It delivered on its promise. It got him out of his small Pennsylvania coal town into the bigger world. Proof was there through the huge door – Africa! A chance to go ashore, drink some beer and party with his friends. Indeed five of them were there together having arranged shore leave for the same hours. Spirits were high as they waited in line to sign out and take the barge to fleet landing. They really did not know where Mombasa was nor did they care. After seven weeks at sea, liberty provided a welcome break in routine. Adventure awaited ashore.

The Executive Officer, XO as he was called, Captain Miller, second in command of the ship walked by the line of those headed ashore. He joked and spoke to several, wishing them a good time in Mombasa. Then, satisfied that all was in order, he returned to his office. His boss, the skipper, Captain Reuben T. Jones, had already left accompanying the admiral to town for the requisite ceremonial calls. Jones ran the ship which was Admiral Zolick's flagship. The admiral headed the task force of which the carrier was the centerpiece. Even though aboard the same ship, by the time they became senior such men had learned the command and responsibilities dance. They were careful not to step on each other's toes. Miller too knew his job. He made the place hum and ensured that everyone stayed busy. He believed that busy men were better sailors. Good morale meant better performance. Morale would be boosted by time ashore. Men would return buoyed up and ready for another stint at sea.

Miller remembered asking his team what bad results could be expected from Mombasa. His chief medical officer said that a number of cases of STDs could be expected, maybe a few cases of malaria as well. He confided that the navy did not yet have a metric for the contraction of AIDS, which might not show up for months in any case. He said he did not expect any heroin or cocaine overdoses, because the available drug in Kenya was marijuana. The security officer stated that the advance team had arranged for police dogs to be present at fleet landing when sailors arrived. He chuckled noting that the dogs were only trained for crowd control, but nevertheless the sailors would assume they were drug sniffers and thus should have a deterrent effect when they returned later that evening. He added that there would probably be some arrests over the next few days, but nothing that preparations in place could not handle.

Preparations

Monica preened in the mirror. She saw her chocolate face and twinkling eyes as she carefully applied some very red lipstick. In looking at the sophisticated woman looking back at her, she could not help but remember how far she'd come. Her pitiful little village, a slum really, just outside Nyeri, a town in central Kenya, was a world away. Her momma still lived there, but Monica fled as soon as she could to escape from the grinding poverty, days with almost nothing to eat, only a dress or two, no school because of no school fees, and worst of all a series of her momma's men who craved the daughter as they had the mother. Raped at ten, she was brutalized and de-sensitized even as she fell into the life of prostitution. Gradually she learned how to tease and please. Kenyan men, even poor ones, lusted after school girls – increasingly because they were deemed to be free of AIDS - so she played that role of innocence, but as her body matured and her eyes became worldlier she attracted fewer of that sort of customer.

Friends in the trade suggested that she go to the city, Nairobi or Mombasa, while she was still young in order to make more money from richer men or even wazungu tourists. Many of those men she was told craved a taste of an African woman along with their beach trip or visit to a game park. With little hesitation, Monica boarded a bus and headed for Mombasa.

Her room was a tawdry cell with a small window high up in one wall. She had pasted several pictures cut from a Kenyan fashion magazine on the walls, but had no furniture other than a single bed, a straight back chair and a locked metal trunk where she kept some clothes and costume jewelry. Several dresses hung on pegs in the wall. Monica thought the room luxurious. She kept it clean. There was electricity for light, a sink with a cold water faucet and an indoor toilet down the hall. Behind the building was a concrete slab courtyard where she and others could dry their wash. The courtyard also sported a kitchen shed where residents could light their small charcoal stoves and cook. It was communal living with both the friendships and quarrels of folks in close quarters. However, by and large Monica got on well with her neighbors. Monica's room was not a place of business. She'd learned early on to keep that separate.

She did not know exactly what to expect from the impending arrival of thousands of sailors, but other hookers told her that business would be brisk and prices were always jacked up - $50 or more and U.S. to boot. Monica was determined to make the best of the opportunity. Her plan was to cruise the terrace and bar of the Castle Hotel on the main street, Kilindini Road. That's where the buses that shuttled the sailors to and from the ports deposited them. Pickings, she hoped would be good. Even though it was early afternoon, she slipped her high heels into a bag - she'd put them on later – and started out.

"Ah la," Raymond the building watchman called out to her as she left, "Going to promote friendship with Americans," he cackled. Monica smiled grimly, but did not bother to reply. He always needled her in an unfriendly manner.

Indeed most Kenyans held very low opinions of women in Monica's profession. Kenya purported to be a very moral society, due both to tribal traditions that carefully regulated sexual relationships and greatly compounded by the influence of ardent Christian missionaries who instilled feverent anti-sin beliefs. Prostitution was a grievous sin and prostitutes considered evil tramps, the dregs of society, disgraces to their families and communities. Yet Monica and her colleagues never wanted for work. They had as many Kenyan clients as foreigners.

The scene at the Castle Hotel was already hectic. Hundreds of men, most in blue jeans and tee shirts, jammed the terrace. Waiters hurried forth to deliver another round of chilled Tusker beers. Curio vendors hawked their carvings of antelopes, crocodiles, elephants and every other variety of wild animal along with larger carved masks or statues of Masaai warriors. There were many takers. Taxi drivers stood on the curb with doors open seeking clients. Other working girls, decked out like Monica in short skirts and tight tops, sashayed through the crowd trying to draw attention, saying hello and asking for a beer. They too found takers.

Monica parried a few, "Not now darlings," and a couple of caresses to her butt as she moved about, then was beckoned to join a table of several men already chatting up Wanjeri, a girl she knew casually. They opened a beer for her and engaged in some patter about Africa. Soon, one of the men said, "Let's go girls. Take us to someplace private." So she, Wanjeri and two of the men jumped into a taxi. She told the driver to take them to a little hotel near the train station. It was a place she used for business and the manager knew she would probably be coming. He expected his share of the business to be good as well.

The Taita Guest House was a dive. It consisted of two floors – four rooms each – above a housewares shop. There was no sign, no reception desk, no one on duty and only a dusty entrance to the steps, but the premises were well known to a small group of prostitutes, Monica among them, who used the building for business. Salim, a taxi cab driver, hung out in the street nearby ready for fares from departing clients from Taita and other such establishments on the block.

In fact, it was Salim who drove Wanjeri's and Monica's two sailors back to the Castle Hotel late that afternoon. An hour or so later just after dark, he also returned the two women To the Castle Hotel. He later commented that they were happy and joking, pleased to have already turned a trick and banked good fees.

Nyali

I got home about four. It had indeed been a busy day, but everything had gone as planned. The sailors got the old folks home painted. Others delivered supplies to the city health clinic, where we all got photographed doing good for tomorrow's paper. Calls on officials went swimmingly. We saw the Provincial Commissioner, the Mayor and the Brigadier. Yes, Kenya's Navy was commanded by a Brigadier General, a practice that dated from first President Jomo Kenyatta's confusion over a plethora of military ranks. After he complained, both Navy and Air Force personnel converted to army ranks. This was particularly amusing from time to time when visiting U.S. naval personnel were introduced to a Kenyan Navy captain. They expected a crusty old veteran, but instead met a young, wet-behind-the-ears officer.

Anyhow, I was back in time to ensure that arrangements for that evening's reception were in place. Of course, everything was prepared. My wife Carol, house staff and the caterer from the nearby Nyali Beach Hotel rarely missed a beat...and if they did, what could I do about it? I took a shower, opened a beer and played Candy Land with the kids.

My guests soon arrived; Admiral Zolick and his team, Captain Jones and his, Brigadier Serumaga and his, Mombasa's consular corps – all of whom except me and the Indian assistant high commissioner were honorary – the honorary consuls being a wide assortment of folks from the shipping, business and tourism communities. There was also a sprinkling of politicians and other elites. I always tried to invite some interesting women, because sailors, even old ones, enjoyed conversations with females after months at sea.

Both the naval visitors and my own staff reported no untoward incidents so far, but we all knew the night was young. There was lots of chit chat about this and that, safaris, ships and sales. The party was a success.

I ate pancakes with the family in the morning before seeing the boys off to school. My drive into the city was perfunctory. Everything was normal. There was the usual congestion around the city market as suppliers pushed carts loaded with vegetables into the old covered edifice. There was a din of noise, but that was expected. I recalled being chastised by a couple of folks once to the effect that when the US Navy visited, they bought all the produce, leaving nothing for city residents. I made a mental note to remember that the market was full, if the topic ever came up again. It was early still and the streets were largely empty of American visitors. I did observe that the stalls of curio vendors near the Catholic Cathedral were overflowing with carvings and that the hawkers were ready to pounce.

In the office, Randle the visiting NIS guy told me that several drunks had been collected by the joint Kenya Police/Shore Patrol teams overnight and had been returned to their ships. I prepared a short cable for Nairobi and Washington recounting the official meetings and noting that the visit was going fine.

In the early afternoon, Catherine buzzed and said that Randle was there and needed to see me.

"What's up? I asked.

"I was just over at the central police station," he replied, "and they got a report in mid-morning of a death, apparently of a prostitute. The bad news is that she was last seen with an American sailor."

"Bad news indeed. Our worst nightmare come true. Any details?" I queried.

"No, not yet. The investigators had just left for the crime scene. They wouldn't let me go with them. I came back so I could get word out to the ships. I will stay in touch with the police and we will cooperate and coordinate as asked."

"OK," I agreed. "Keep me in the loop. You have my numbers here and at home. Call anytime. I'll alert the embassy and think about press points. I know that the ambassador will want only one point for press contact and that will be either me or our press spokesman in Nairobi. Understood?"

"Affirmative, we want to stay far away from the papers. I don't want to put this on our port radio net, so I'm off to fleet landing and out to the ship."

Randle hurried out. I took a deep breath and phoned my boss, Peter Hawkins, the DCM in Nairobi. He greeted me cheerfully, but sobered up quickly when I related the problem. I added, "There will be hue and cry here when the American sailor connection is revealed. Memories of the Bellinger case will reverberate. We'll be judged guilty, right off the bat."

He agreed, "Obviously, there's gonna be lots of politics in this. It looks like we're in for some interesting times. We'll handle the press from here. Make sure the navy understands that."

"Gotcha, I'll keep you posted." I promised.

The Scene

About nine o'clock that morning, James Ndaka made his rounds at the Taita Guest House collecting for the previous nights' stays. There was no response from his knocking on Monica's second floor door. He banged harder, still no response. He tried the door, found it open, so peered in. "Hodi, hodi" he called, Swahili roughly for is anyone here? There was no response. He noticed a woman's figure on the bed, covered up. He checked. She was dead, blood and froth coming from her mouth.

Ndaka was no fool. He quickly left. He rushed downstairs and over to the Central Police Station several blocks away. He reported the death to the constable on duty; told how and why he had found the body. The desk officer in turn ordered two constables to return to the scene with Ndaka to verify the finding. They did. As the bad news spread, they also learned from Salim, the taxi cab driver, that Monica, a prostitute, had entertained probably two American sailors the day before. Subsequently, investigators were dispatched.

Inspector Oyugi was the first on the scene and took charge. The girl was obviously dead. So he began a systematic look at the room while waiting for the forensic team to show up. The allegation that an American was involved clearly raised the profile of what might otherwise be an unremarkable case. Was she murdered? If so, by whom?

The room was basic, a single bed, a table, and some clothes on the floor. Monica's body, however, was oddly placed. She was nude under the cover. Her legs were spread apart and each foot caught in the metal springs underneath the skimpy mattress. It did not look like a natural position. Her head faced upward and bloody foam spittle had dried on her mouth. Under the bed was an empty pack of Marlboro cigarettes and an empty package of durex condoms. Clothes were piled on top of a purse. Along with other items, there were 112 shillings and one fifty dollar bill in the purse.

Oyugi remarked to himself that was a considerable sum of money and the fact that it remained in the purse was evidence that robbery was not the motive.

Oyugi left the room and questioned the two women who stood anxiously in the hallway. Maria Kyalo said that the dead woman's name was Monica Njere, from somewhere near Nyeri. She had been in Mombasa for several months and was in the sex trade. Florence confirmed Maria's identification. She added that she had briefly seen a white man leave the room about 10:00 the previous night. Asked if she could identify him, she said she had not seen him very clearly, but he was short and lightly built.

Oyugi was interrupted at this point by the arrival of the forensics team. They photographed the scene, collected the cigarette and condom packages. They cut and bagged Monica's nails as possible evidence of a struggle, then removed the body to the morgue at Coast General Hospital. They boxed the clothes, purse and other items for further perusal.

The inspector resumed interrogation of folks around the house. Most productive were recollections by Salim. He stated that he drove Monica to the Castle Hotel about dark. An hour or so later, back outside the Taita house, he saw her arrive with a white man in tow. Then about ten thirty, a white man, he could not say if it was the same one who went into the establishment with Monica or not, came out and asked for a ride "back to the ship." The man said that he did not have much money. He gave Salim fifteen shillings, but then added a silver zippo lighter with the crest "USS America" on the side. Salim agreed and took him down to Kilindini port entrance. No, the man said this is not it. Salim said he realized that the man wanted to go to the fleet landing at Mbaraki wharf. Salim said that he deposited the guy at the Castle Hotel where he could catch a shuttle bus, rather than take him out to Mbaraki. Asked to describe him, Salim said he wore a white tee shirt and had hairy arms. He was not a big man, even smaller than Kenyans. Oyugi took the lighter into evidence.

Samuel , the night watchman who guarded several buildings on the street, agreed with the fact that a white man had come out of Taita about ten thirty. He described him as slight of build with sandy hair and a mustache. He was wearing a yellow striped shirt. Samuel added that the man was sweating and seemed to be in a hurry. He saw him negotiate with Salim and then go off in the taxi.

A third man also stepped forward. He said his name was James. He had a room on the third floor. He said when coming in he passed a white guy trotting down the stairs. He recalled the man wore a white shirt and blue jeans. He added that he really had not seen him well.

Wrapping up for the time being at the Taita Guest House location, Pius Oyugi reflected that finding a suspect and then indentifying him would be difficult. Yet, that was his job and this case would garner the spotlight, so he redoubled his determination to succeed. He returned to the station to brief his superiors.

Oyugi and his boss, Provincial Police Commissioner Jacob Kapila, reviewed the sparse information available and outlined the next steps. Oyugi was instructed to contact the American liaison officer to seek his assistance in identifying the "white man" who was a person of interest in the death. Kapila then telephoned the state prosecutor Simon Mbai to alert him and also to request that Mbai alert the Attorney General's office in Nairobi. Kapila immediately placed another call to his superior at national police headquarters in Nairobi.

The next afternoon at Coast General Hospital, coroner Dr. Mohamed, examined the body. He concluded that death was by asphyxia due to strangulation. He reported a bruise to the left side of the face, a small cut above the eye, blood and froth coming from the mouth and nose. He noted that the tongue had been bitten and the eyes were bloodshot. He said there was no evidence of injuries around the genitals. He estimated that time of death to be about 30 hours previously or about 3:00 am on April 6, plus or minus two hours.

Cooperation

Randle checked in with me mid-afternoon. He advised that the navy was prepared to cooperate to the fullest with local authorities. They did not want to blemish their reputation by seeming to duck. Certainly, as Captain Jones stated, "if one of his men was guilty of murder, justice should prevail." I was relieved but not surprised with this confirmation. It is what I expected. After seeing me, Randle went back to the central police station.

Oyugi collared him as soon as he arrived. He related what he knew. The girl was dead, probably murdered, although the coroner's conclusions had not yet been received. Oyugi reviewed the scene and especially the incriminating evidence of a white man with a USS America lighter. "How can we find that man?" Oyugi asked.

Randle asked, "Are there witnesses? Can anyone identify him? Do you have a name?"

Oyugi replied, "No name, but several witnesses – one woman inside the house, three men outside, a watchman, a hanger-on and the taxi driver who drove him back to the Castle – claim they saw him. We'd normally do a line-up for identification, but we need the suspect for that. If the man in question was a sailor – and I am sure he was- and if he did go back to his ship – as he probably did, then how can the police here in town figure out who he is?"

"Valid issues," Randle replied. "I've been instructed to provide all possible help. Perhaps we could take the witnesses out to the carrier. We'd parade men matching the description by and they could take a look. Would that help?"

"Sounds like all we've got," Oyugi agreed.

Time was moving on and both men had arrangements to make. They decided to set the event for the next morning beginning at 9:00 when Oyugi and the witnesses would arrive at Mbaraki pier.

Randle hustled out to the carrier and conferred with the security team there. XO Miller said, "This is highly irregular. Could a witness really pick someone out of the thousands of men on board?

Randle shrugged, "It depends on how well they saw him and on how well they remember." He added, "I was instructed to offer fullest cooperation. This seemed to be the only avenue open. I personally doubt that a suspect will be identified, but we ought to proceed. The consul told me that the politics of this are already hot, but if the Navy were deemed to be covering up, then all hell would break loose. "

Miller conceded the point and gave permission for the parade to be organized.

Evidence

Back at the station Oyugi collected the box of items from the crime scene and took it to his desk. Before studying the items, a glance at a photo taped to the wall reminded him of how far he had come. It was a group shot of seven men standing in front of a beached fishing boat. The portrait was of Oyugi's family, father, brothers and cousins, taken a couple of years back when he went home for his uncle's funeral. He stood on the left easily distinguished by his city dress. Home was Homa Bay, a fishing community on the shores of Lake Victoria Nyanza, Kenya's huge inland sea. Oyugi's family was fishermen of the Luo tribe. They spent long days and nights casting, setting and drawing nets in the lake. The payoff was traditionally meager, fresh fish did not last long in Kenya's tropical climate and sun drying them was onerous work as well. Even so, Oyugi's father sent all his children, even daughters, to primary school, but only one, Pius himself, had demonstrated the acumen to advance further. Education was a huge family investment and was granted only to an accomplished student. Pius was the one chosen by his father to continue. After primary school he attended Kisumu Boys' High School. He did well enough there to earn his certificate, but not well enough to gain admittance to university. A police recruiter had visited the school during his last year looking to induce educated young men into a special entry program that would move them, if they were successful, into the upper ranks of the police. His classmates were skeptical because police work was viewed as an inferior occupation, but Pius seized the opportunity. He never regretted it. After a stint of learning the ropes, he had progressed steadily up the ladder. Now he was the newly minted chief inspector in Mombasa, a position of some importance.

His reflections aside Oyugi turned his attention to the box from the crime scene. He pulled out the items of clothing. The victim had been a large woman, not fat, but certainly not small. The dark blue dress, the only one, so presumably the one she wore on the night of her death had a foreign label in it. Oyugi was not surprised by that. He assumed that it had been acquired on the used clothing market. Most Kenyans bought used clothing, especially fancy dresses and such exported from rich countries like the U.S. and the U.K. He had been told once that used clothing was among Kenya's largest imports. The shoes were well worn black flats. Yet the fact that she wore real shoes rather than rubber sandals, indicated that the girl aspired to some standards.

Oyugi spilled out the contents of the purse. Unlike the dress the purse itself was well worn, the hasp did not even clasp properly. A Kenyan identity card inscribed with the name Monica Njere was accompanied by a poor photo. Oyugi had no reason to doubt that it was the deceased's. A small change purse contained the 112 shillings

Oyugi counted out at the crime scene – two fifties, a ten and two one shilling coins – plus the American fifty dollar bill. All together this was a sizable sum. Oyugi guessed that an American must have provided the $50 bill, but the shillings represented the price of several local customers. Fingering the bills, the inspector reiterated his conclusion that robbery could not have been the motive. This was money enough to kill for, but it remained intact. Oyugi carefully entered the serial numbers of the bills into the inventory list. He underlined a mental note to ensure that the money got to the deceased's family.

Other items on the desk included a comb and a tube of red lipstick. There was also a small booklet only about two inches by three. Oyugi opened it. On the first page was written the name of Monica Njere and an address in Mombasa that was not the Taita Guest House. A good lead, Oyugi suspected that was Monica's real abode. He would check it out. The next two pages had some names and phone numbers. In reading them one surprised him - that of Bile H. Bile was a Somali name. Why would a Kikuyu whore have a Somali client? And why, Oyugi wondered would she have a name that resembled, at least at first glance, a man named Bile Hussien who was wanted by authorities? Mulling over that coincidence Oyugi knew that this piece of information, if valuable at all, would have to be assessed by the Special Branch.

The inspector reached for his phone. His party answered immediately, "Okoth here." Oyugi identified himself. "Samuel, it is me Pius. Listen I have just run into something that might be interesting, can I drop over to share it with you?

"Pius, you have certainly piqued my interest. Sure come right on over."

Within ten minutes inspector Oyugi was climbing the stairs in the Provincial Administration building to the third floor office of the Special Branch, Kenya's secret police. Samuel Okoth, the Mombasa representative waved him to a chair. The two were fellow Luo tribesmen. Futhermore Okoth had been two years ahead of Oyugi at Kisumu Boys High. Only acquaintances there, they had become friends when both found themselves posted to Mombasa, alien tribal territory for two westerners. They socialized regularly together and with other Luos mostly over beer in the evenings. As a policeman Oyugi knew the general purview of the Special Branch, but had not previously had occasion to do business with the organization.

Oyugi began, "Samuel, I have seen the circulars asking for help in finding specific people, especially those radical Somalis. In reviewing some evidence from a murder scene I ran across the name of Bile H. and a phone number. It occurred to me that it might refer to Bile Hussein, one of the most wanted. I cannot figure why there might be a link between a Kikuyu prostitute and a man on your list, but I wanted to inform you about it."

"Wow," Okoth replied, "I'm interested. Tell me about the murder. Do you think this Bile H. was involved?"

Oyugi related the tale of the crime as he thought it probably happened. A drunk American sailor took it out on a prostitute. He elaborated on the booklet he found and the names and numbers in it. He concluded, "The evidence and witness statements point to an American sailor as being the killer. I don't think that Bile H., whoever he is, was there. I'll leave it to you to follow up that lead. Please let me know, if anything comes of it."

The Storm

All hell broke loose overnight. Kenya's leading newspaper, The Nation's morning headline screamed "American Sailor Kills Kenyan Girl." The story tracked the facts as we knew them: a dead girl, a prostitute, last seen with a sailor from the USS America. It noted that the Kenyan Police were seized with the investigation in which US Navy authorities were cooperating. The paper reminded readers of the debacle of Bellinger case and expressed the necessity this time to see justice delivered so as to adequately punish the guilty man.

"It looks carefully planted," I told Randle as he reviewed plans for the excursion to the carrier. At his request I had arranged for a Swahili interpreter from the American side to accompany the group. For that task I had called on Abdul Jaffer, a courtly Swahili gentleman, my Swahili coach and friend, who had once taught for several years at the Defense Language Institute in California. He did not see any up-side to participation, but out of friendship had agreed.

Catherine gave me a stack of phone messages – most were from local reporters from Kenyan papers, but the AP guy from Nairobi had called as had the BBC from London. I reiterated that Catherine should advise that all press queries were being handled by the embassy spokesman in Nairobi.

I called the embassy in Nairobi to review the bidding. Hawkins told me the press line was as discussed: straightforward acknowledgment that the U.S. Navy was cooperating with the Kenya Police in the investigation. Nothing much beyond that. I surmised that the leak to the Nation was from the police; presumably so they could pin blame on the Navy when the investigation turned up empty-handed. Meanwhile the gratuitous publicity would only hamper efforts to uncover facts.

I told Hawkins that the shore team had departed for the carrier for the identification parade, but we wouldn't know results for several hours.

On the USS America

Oyugi arrived at Mbaraki pier with three witnesses, only the men, and two other inspectors. He expressed confidence that witnesses would be able to identify the suspect. Abdul reported to me later that the three were quiet and obviously intimidated by what was happening. The ride out was bumpy and the transfer to the mighty ship scary – jumping onto a metal platform from a bobbing boat.

Once aboard, the Kenyan group was led to a large cafeteria room that had been reconfigured for the identity parade. Each witness was seated by himself at the outside of a U where they could not see each other. The parade line would pass before them. An initial screening had been made by the ship's security personnel. Only white guys of relatively small stature were included. This reduced the number of participants to a thousand or so. Also, since this was the carrier's second day in port and liberty rotated, none of those ashore during the identification parade that morning would have been on the beach the day/night of the killing.

The walk-by began. The men began to pass. Randle asked Abdul to pay attention to Salim as he seemed most convinced of his own view, but it was Samuel who tentatively identified two men as seeming to resemble the man he saw. At the end of the hour and a half exercise, Salim made no identifications nor did James.

The two sailors that Samuel fingered were quickly pulled aside by security personnel. Both claimed to have been on duty aboard on the night in question. A check of the liberty records and confirmation from their supervisors verified their statements. They were ruled out.

Oyugi, his constables, the three witnesses and Adbul sat desultorily on sofas in the officers' mess waiting for transport ashore. Oyugi was disappointed that no viable suspect had been found. The witnesses were probably contemplating how they would deal with angry police officials.

Meanwhile, after seeing the exercise off to a start, XO Miller retired to his cabin/office to catch up on some paperwork. After an hour or so, two men knocked on the door, saying they were there to fix the toilet. Miller concurred, but noting the smallish size of the two, asked if they had participated in the identity parade. Neither had and neither appeared to be aware of it. They said they had been on a job during the morning muster.

"Come with me," the XO ordered. He led them to the cafeteria, but the event was over. He was directed to the officers' mess. Miller conferred with Randle there advising that these two men had missed the parade. Randle then asked Abdul to convey that to the witnesses. "Did one of them fit the description?"

"Ndio,"said Salim, "ni komma yeye," (Yes, it's like him.) pointing to the man that would be identified as Jim Tyrell. Oyugi was euphoric. We've got our man, he thought. Salim's observation was translated for Randle.

As with the others previously identified, Tyrell was grilled by two security agents. It turned out that he had been ashore at the time in question and that he stopped by the Castle Hotel. He was adamant however, that he spent the whole time in town with friends from the ship who could vouch for their movements. Tyrell said they had gone from the big hotel in town where the bus dropped them off (the Castle) to the Oceanic Hotel, where they had rented a room, taken a swim, gambled in the casino and eaten dinner. He met a hooker in the bar afterwards. She asked, "Do you want to love me?" Tyrell, the girl, his buddy Latham and another girl, then went up to their room, #216. Another of the navy men was passed out in one bed, so the two sailors used the other two beds. After making love, Tyrell showered. About this time, 11 or so, the other friends came to the room. Tyrell woke the sleeping drunk and the two of them went downstairs, leaving the girls and other men to sort out the room. At the hotel entrance Tryell and Whitesides met four other sailors from the America. The six of them shared a taxi back to Mbaraki pier where he signed in.

As soon as Jim revealed the names of his buddies, NIS agents sought them out and sequestered them for questioning. In sworn statements, each in his own way repeated the narrative that Tyrell shared. There were enough minor discrepancies – times of movements for example – and additional details such as Smith rented the room and later phoned his wife, who loaned who money, etc. so that the experienced NIS agents believed that the collective story was honest and accurate. They were convinced that it was a not an alibi concocted by friends to shield Tyrell.

Randle told me later that based on Tyrell's explanation of his movements in Mombasa, fully corroborated by others, that Tyrell should have been exonerated at that time. Were he in charge of the investigation, Randle confided he would have moved on at that point.

Oyugi had listened to Tyrell's statement and was briefed on the corroborating statements and the NIS opinion that Tyrell was not involved in the prostitute's death. Randle promised to provide copies of the sworn statements within hours. Oyugi nodded, but stated only that he would have to review the evidence with his superiors.

The police party then left the carrier.

Upon return ashore Abdul, the interpreter, came to see me as I had earlier requested to provide a read-out of what transpired. He was not in the loop regarding Tyrell's statement, but did provide atmospherics regarding the witnesses and Kenyan police behavior. Adbul observed that everyone, himself included, was overwhelmed by the size of the ship and the thousands of people on board. He said that Navy personnel were welcoming and professional. He detected no bad vibes from them. In contrast, he said that the witnesses had been bullied by Oyugi before the trip and instructed by him that they were to find the murderer. Even so, Abdul carefully noted that no specific identification was made. No "that's him. That's the man I saw." Instead all three identifications - two by Samuel and one by Salim - translated from Swahili were "that looks like him."

Abdul noted that after the parade was over and they were sitting on a sofa elsewhere. The witnesses were cowed by their failure. Then an officer brought in two more men and pointedly asked if either of them was the one. Abdul said that while that may have been the American way of seeing that every "t" was crossed, to the Kenyans it was a clear signal to choose one. "So," Abdul sighed, "Salim did." Abdul added that Oyugi too may have read more into the late presentation than was intended. Even though he was grasping at straws all along, the offering up of a suspect at the end indicated to him more knowledge on the

American side than it was revealing. "Oyugi's not done," Abdul said in closing.

I spent a few minutes organizing my thoughts before calling Hawkins in Nairobi. Ambassador Starke joined the call. I related happenings aboard the carrier as I understood them. I noted that only one of the three identified seamen had been ashore on the night in question. Inspector Oyugi had his name, but despite Tyrell's acceptable counter story, I thought Oyugi was likely to pursue the investigation with him as the focus.

"Good report," the Ambassador responded. "Write it up for us soonest. This case is drawing attention in Washington, especially from the Navy. I will need to see the Minister of Foreign Affairs on it, perhaps tomorrow."

"Yes, sir, I will get a cable out within the hour. "

Confabs

At six that evening, just as the sun was beginning to drop and the shadows lengthening, a black Mercedes limousine pulled up to the gate at State House in Nairobi. Despite the ministerial plaque on the front, the conscientious guard stuck his head in the driver's window to verify that the passenger was indeed the Attorney General. Upon verification, he backed a step or two and popped a magnificent salute. Amos Makupa grinned. He always liked to be shown respect.

Descending at the front entrance, the AG was met by an usher and led to the small conference room. The Foreign Minister and the Commissioner of Police were already there. Shortly, Jonah Cheruiyot, Minister of State at the Presidency walked in. Shaking hands around, he got right down to business.

"Philip," he addressed the commissioner, "what is this news from Mombasa that we need to consider?"

"You saw the Nation this morning. That story is correct. There has been a murder, probably by an American sailor. There was an effort out on the ship this afternoon to identify a suspect, but it was only partially successful. "

"What do you mean by partially?" the AG interrupted.

"Well, apparently only one of the three eyewitnesses picked a man. Yet we now have a name, so the decision we must make is whether or not to proceed."

"I reviewed the agreement with the U.S. prior to coming over," AG Makupa advised, "and with regard to military personnel, Kenya has jurisdiction over felonies such as murder committed in Kenya. So, we're clear on that ground. However, more troublesome is the process by which the suspect was identified. Our law is clear about how a line-up should function. A walk about aboard a foreign naval ship would hardly seem acceptable. "

"There's more," the commissioner observed wryly, "the suspect in question put forth an alibi that was corroborated by shipmates. But," he raised his hand to forestall objections, "my police inspectors believe it to be a concocted story."

Retaking the floor, Cheruiyot said, "I take it then we are on satisfactory legal grounds to proceed. That's good, because the issue is political. After that Bellinger case a couple of years ago, the government cannot be seen by the people to be soft on American sailors. The press is already harping on this point. If the man is guilty, this time he must hang."

"Political it is," the Foreign Minister interjected, "but not just domestically. The Americans are sticklers for proper process. If Kenya prosecutes and convicts an innocent man, then hangs him to boot, there will be difficulties. Not just with the Americans, but with other important donors as well. We need to tread very carefully. My view would be that if the identification is flimsy, that we let it go now."

"Objection," the commissioner interjected, "we cannot drop this without going through all the process. If in the end the man is innocent, our courts can decide."

"Yeah, like they did the Bellinger case," Cheruiyot scoffed, "they found him guilty, then let him go."

"This time, I will ensure that a better judge is assigned," stated Makupa.

Cheruiyot, said, "Okay then we will proceed. Phillip tell your men to go ahead, arrest this man and find out whether his story is valid." Turning to the Foreign Minister, he added, "Robert, we count on you to keep the Americans mollified and assured that due process is being pursued. They have been helpful so far, and their cooperation will remain essential. We don't want to alienate them. Phillip, caution the police investigators to scrupulously follow procedures with regard to the sailor."

With murmured assents the meeting broke up.

Arrest

Senior Chief Woodley and NIS agent Randle briefed me the next morning. Senior Chief reported that all provisioning and fuel bunkering had been accomplished. Two 141 flights had discharged cargo and mail for the ships, both airport and port operations had gone well. Randle added that it had been an unusually quiet night on the liberty front, everyone seemed to be on their best behavior in wake of the murder allegation. Senior Chief said that the battle fleet would sail in the late afternoon.

I asked," If Tyrell's aboard, then it's over?"

"Affirmative," Randle responded.

Randle was back within the hour to advise that Oyugi demanded that Tyrell be brought ashore for further questioning. He added that he had passed the request to the captain of the USS America along with the recommendation that it be agreed to.

"How would that work?" I asked.

"I've thought about it," he answered, " the Ajax, a tender, is not part of the battle group and was staying another day or so anyway. Tryell can be transferred to the Ajax temporarily. From there we can make him available to the police for their investigation."

"Okay," I agreed, "keep me in the loop."

Again I phoned embassy Nairobi. Hawkins advised that the ambassador had been called to the Foreign Ministry urgently; presumably about the murder case.

Indeed that turned out to be true. Ambassador Starke called me to say that the minister had clearly stated that Kenya would pursue this case properly, carefully respectful of the legal provisions of due process. He asked that I convey that message and his belief in the accuracy of it to Captain Jones. I agreed to do so. I updated the ambassador on developments in Mombasa, especially the plans being made to transfer the suspect to another ship so he could stay on.

"All the more important," he retorted, "to convey my message to Captain Jones."

Senior Chief had radio contact from his office to the purser on board the America. They quickly rigged up a connection to Captain Jones and I relayed the ambassador's message. Jones seemed somewhat reassured by this, but apparently still smelled a skunk.

"Are you sure this is on the up and up?" he asked, "I don't want to see one of my men railroaded into a death sentence."

"I share your apprehensions," I replied honestly, "this is being driven politically. There probably needs to be more show before it can wind down." I did not want to express my fear that Tyrell would indeed lose his life as a scapegoat to public pressure.

By late morning, Tyrell had been transferred to the Ajax. Fleet landing at Mbaraki closed at 2:00 pm. All hands were aboard the ships berthed in Kilindini by 4:00 pm. The USS America battle fleet sailed just before sunset. In the distance the carrier's big anchor rattled home dripping sea grass as the accompanying destroyers and cruisers cut seaward through the cool blue water of the Kilindini channel. With my wife and little boys I joined the spectators on the seafront to wave as the line of ships departed. Before long the ships disappeared into the dusk.

Investigation

Randle was a consummate professional. Once Tyrell had been left behind, he ordered two things to be done. First was to take a detailed statement from the sailor, one that would complement his explanation of his movements on the night in question. Second was to ask that a navy polygraph expert be sent to examine the man and his statement. Randle believed that these two devices would clearly identify the veracity of his alibi. Randle had agent Loffton take the statement that evening aboard the Ajax.

Randle later gave me a copy of Tyrell's statement. It opened with identification both of the suspect and of special agent Loffton who took the statement. It noted that Tyrell had been advised of his rights and was making the statement voluntarily, the signed waiver was attached. Tyrell described himself as weighing 159 pounds, 70 inches tall, blond hair, blue eyes and having a tattoo on each shoulder.

Tyrell stated that approximately 1130 on April 5 he departed the USS America via a navy contracted local boat. He wore blue jeans and a beige V neck shirt with a collar. He advised that he also brought along a burgundy tee shirt with a front pocket. He had $25 in U.S. currency.

With him on the same water taxi were friends Tom Latham, Earl Whitesides, Joe Davis and Chuck Smith. They disembarked at the landing near the ferry (later determined to be Mbaraki pier near Likoni Ferry). They got on a navy chartered bus that stopped at a hotel (later determined to be the Castle). All on the bus but the five of them got off there. Tyrell's group got off at the next stop and walked up a short hill to the Mission to Seaman's Club. It was very crowded, so they stayed only a few minutes. Tyrell suggested that they go to the Oceanic Hotel that they had seen from the water taxi. The five hired a red taxi and went there arriving about 1300. He and Whitesides went directly to the bar. They had no intention of renting a room as

Whitesides had duty the following morning and Tyrell had only $25. However, Smith, Latham and Davis rented a room, no. 216. In the bar Whitesides bought at least two rounds of beers before Tyrell went to the lobby to exchange his money for shillings. He returned to the bar. The other men came in wearing swimming trunks and advised they had rented a room and were going for a swim. Whitesides borrowed the key and Tyrell accompanied him to the room. Whitesides changed into trunks, but Tyrell did not have any. They joined the others at the pool.

After a while Davis left to place a phone call to his wife in the U.S. Whitesides and Latham went to get something to eat leaving only Smith and Tyrell at the pool. Soon they too went into the restaurant to eat. Because the other men were about finished, they sat at a separate table. After eating he and Smith went to the desk to get the room key. The receptionist told them she had a call for room 216. They assumed it was for Davis, so went out to the pool to tell him. Davis spoke on the phone from the lobby. Afterwards the five decided to go to check out the town. They took a mini-bus cab to the Castle Hotel He believed it was about 1530. They sat on the back terrace and immediately a lot of black girls began to join them. Tyrell recalled that one of the girls sat on the arm of his chair and kept playing around with him. She put his hand on her leg which he described as hairy. Tyrell said that other ship mates joined them at their table. Meanwhile he managed to get rid of the girl. During the course of a couple of hours there, Tyrell said that Whitesides, Latham and possibly Smith had left for a time with females.

Tyrell said that he, Davis and Holt, a shipmate who joined them, sat there and fended off women until his shipmates returned. They then decided to return to the Oceanic Hotel, but Holt declined to go with them. Just as it was getting dark, the five left in a taxi and went straight to the Oceanic casino. Tyrell recalled that they had to sign an admission book at the entrance. Tyrell claimed that he lost 150 shillings at blackjack leaving him with only about 10 shillings.

After about an hour in the casino, the group left and went to the hotel entering through the main entrance. He and Latham went into the bar. They drank beer and played the pinball machine. When Smith came in, Tyrell said he borrowed 100 shillings from him. He advised that while purchasing a beer at the bar, a girl engaged him in conversation. This same girl asked him to introduce his friend (Latham) to her girlfriend, which he did. After a short time the two girls indicated that they wanted the men to take them to bed. The girl he was talking to indicated there would be no charge, so he agreed.

Tyrell went to get the key from the desk while the women followed Latham to the stairs. There they were stopped by hotel employees. Tyrell came over showed the key and advised that the women were with him. They were allowed to go up. He recalled the time was approximately 2100.

Upon entering room 216 Tyrell saw that Whitesides was lying on a bed fully clothed. He asked him to leave, but Whitesides rolled over and said he was asleep. The two couples got undressed. Tyrell and his girl took the middle bed and had sexual intercourse. After an hour or so, Tyrell said he and his friend went into the bathroom and took a bath together. When he went back into the bedroom nude, Davis and Smith were there. He asked them to leave. He went back into the bathroom, took the girl her clothes, and when they emerged Smith and Davis had left. Latham and his friend had moved to the balcony. He and the girl lay down again on the bed and before long she removed her pink panties and they had sex again. Afterwards Tyrell said he went by himself into the bathroom and washed. He recalled having a headache and an upset stomach. Tyrell said he told Latham that the girls would have to leave, but Latham said they could stay. Within minutes Davis and Smith knocked again. Tyrell said that he woke up Whitesides and prepared to leave. His girl asked for money so she could go shopping the next day. He claimed to have given her 40 shillings.

Tyrell said that he and Whitesides then went downstairs at approximately 2300 and got into a taxi, but the driver wanted 100 shillings to take them to the water taxi. They did not have enough so got out. Soon they linked up with four sailors they did not know and took a white van to the landing. Tyrell said he paid his last 20 shillings for the ride and the others also paid. He said it rained hard while they waited for the water taxi. They were back aboard the USS America by 0100.

Tyrell described his lady friend to be about five feet six, medium build, 125 pounds, big breasts, short black hair. She wore a yellow blouse and skirt. Her name was Anna, he thought. She said she was 19 from Nairobi only in Mombasa to visit her aunt who lived on the other side of the ferry. Betty was her cousin. Tyrell said he thought she was clean, disease free, but he did not have a condom in any case. He admitted being mistaken in that regard. He said he was treated for gonorrhea on the ship the next day. He described the other girl as big, about 150 pounds but short, only 5 feet 2 inches. She wore a dark dress.

Tyrell said that he smoked Marlboro cigarettes that afternoon while at the Castle which he borrowed from his friends. He did not recall smoking in the Oceanic Hotel room. He said that Latham does not smoke. Tyrell said the last pack of cigarettes he bought was two months ago when preparing for the cruise. He said he did have a lighter with the USS America logo on it. It broke months ago, but might still be in his locker.

There was a citation at the end signed by Special Agent Lofton affirming the accuracy of the document.

Sex Trade

Whew, I thought after reading it. Liberty is a pretty sordid affair; just beer and sex, kind of pitiful actually. But sex was indeed part of the tourist allure of Kenya's coast. European visitors, both men and women, usually middle aged, often looked for "beach bunnies" or "beach boys" for a fling. It was not unusual for these assignations to last for the week or two that the tourists were in country. Generally, the relationship, if you could call it that, ended there - however, not always. I remembered one instance a year past when an American merchant seaman off a McCormick Lines ship came to see me. He was graying, about sixty and well worn. He brought along with him a twenty-something Kenyan girl, who while pretty, was all tarted up. She was obviously a professional prostitute. The man told me that they were in love and intended to marry. He wanted to get her a visa so she could join him in Baltimore once his voyage was finished. I ushered the lady into the outer office and had a man-to-man chat with the sailor. He said that he would be retiring after this last trip. He needed her to care for him. I told him bluntly that she appeared to be a professional sex worker only using him as a mechanism to get to America. Once there I predicted that she would abandon him and move on. No, he protested she was not a hooker, but he conceded that she was looking for a ticket to a better life. If he was that ticket, okay with him. I told him bluntly that I would not recommend a visa for the girl, but in response to his question of how he might proceed, I told him that he would have to file a fiancée's petition with INS in Baltimore. If that was approved, then she could travel. He thanked me and said he would follow up.

I expected the matter to end there; that they would move on. But lo and behold, about six months later the two again paid me a visit. The sailor explained that he had followed up with INS as I advised and had gotten the petition approved. They were off, back to Baltimore in the morning. Although flabbergasted by this resolution, I wished them luck. Of course, I never learned how it turned out. I still hope that she gave him comfort in his old age.

The sex aspect of tourism was one that drew occasional commentary - always of a disgusting nature - in the papers. Writers deplored that money lured young Kenyans into the despicable life style. Other commentators decried overall the impact of tourism wherein rich people reveled in luxury, drink and sport. My German colleague would agree with this observation saying that yes people played during their vacation. That is what vacations were for. The rest of the year they buckled down every day and put in an honest day's work in an often dreary factory. I did accept the validity of his observation for the tourists themselves. Nothing indicated the therapeutic value of a holiday more than the daily changeover at Moi airport. Arrivals trudged gray, glum and quiet from their planes while those departing were tanned, laughing and boisterous.

Nonetheless, critics believed that tourism sent the wrong message to conservative coastal communities about values. Remember that on the predominantly Moslem coast, most people did not drink alcohol at all and women were modestly dressed. Swahili women wore black bui-buis, cloaks that covered their heads and faces. I believed it certainly true that the licentious nature of tourism did undermine traditional societal values, but there was a tradeoff. And it was economic. Kenya's beautiful beaches and magnificent game parks were legitimate attractions that the developing nation was right to exploit. The country needed foreign exchange and its people needed jobs. The issue was how to find the balance. Overall I judged that Kenya did find a decent balance, but the sordid side of the sex trade raised its head from time to time. Certainly, that was a legitimate criticism of ship visits. Prostitutes, professionals and part timers, flocked to Mombasa from all over east Africa when the fleet was in port.

Mombasa

Mombasa had been a port for 600 years or more. It was a cross roads and a melting pot. Thanks to its fine small harbor, it grew into an important trading town by the 13th century. The town (now called Old Town) that grew up beside the harbor, was part of a flourishing coastal culture whose inhabitants – today's Swahilis – were the progeny of Arab, Persians, and Africans. By the late 1400's Mombasa was one of a string of city states of the Zenj Empire that dotted the East African littoral. These cities were oriented to the sea and to trading partners as far away as China. Although the coastal regions behind the island redoubts provided food, they produced little else of economic value.

Europeans arrived in the form of Portuguese explorers seeking routes to the fabled east. Vasco da Gama sailed by Mombasa in 1498, not calling in on account of the fierce reputation of the denizens. Instead he stopped at Malindi, a hundred miles up the coast where he erected a stone cross marking Portuguese interest, prior to sailing on to India. Other Portuguese adventurers followed in his wake. Their weaponry permitted them to seize Swahili towns including Mombasa which was occupied in 1505. In order to consolidate their African empire, the Portuguese fortified the towns. Nothing was as impressive as the massive bastion of Fort Jesus that still dominates the entrance to the old harbor of Mombasa. Intrigue and violence characterized the two hundred years of Portuguese suzerainty. Control of the city passed back and forth several times between the Portuguese and local contenders. At one point the Portuguese contingent inside the fort was under siege for over a year before they broke.

By the end of 17th century, Portuguese sea power was giving way to British and French. Consequently, its hold on the Indian Ocean coast dissolved. Control shifted to the Sultan of Oman. He and his successors crafted a kingdom ruled from Zanzibar but with the connivance of local communities. Scions of prominent Mombasa families jockeyed for control of their region, but within the context of allegiance to the Sultan. Cloves, slaves, ivory and mangrove poles were exported eastward behind the winds of the kaskazi , the north blowing monsoon. The southward blowing winds brought the dhows home six months later.

Intrepid European explorers such as Livingstone, Speke, Burton and Stanley used Zanzibar as their departure point from the 1850's onward. It was the Sultan's capital, well supplied by sea and gave access to the slave caravan routes that crossed Tanganyika. Although Mombasa was increasingly cosmopolitan, its hinterland consisted of harsh dry scrub bush lands on the other side of which lived fierce Masaai warriors. Even so, missionary explorers Krapf and Rebmann established a station at Rabai on the mainland inland from Mombasa and sought to convert the natives. As it began to curtail the slave trade in the Indian Ocean by the middle of the 19th century, British warships freed slaves captured at sea at Freretown on the mainland near Mombasa.

Rebmann ventured inland and in 1849 was the first European to sight Mt. Kilimanjaro. Skeptics at the Royal Geographic Society in London scoffed stating unequivocally that snow could not exist on the equator. In 1885 Joseph Thompson pioneered a route from Mombasa to Lake Victoria (the lake had been named by Speke in 1858). The interior of Kenya began to reveal its splendor to the outside world.

The British assumed power on the Kenyan coast following the demarcation of spheres of influence at Berlin in 1885. In this scramble for Africa, Britain was not initially interested in establishing colonies in Africa, it merely wanted to trade and to deny others, i.e. Germany, control of the sources of the Nile, whose waters were vital to Egypt where the Suez canal (built in 1856)was a vital interest. Pressures from missionaries, explorers and commercial interests that focused on Uganda, however, compelled Britain to assert itself there and in Mombasa. Lord Lugard, who recommended the protectorate over Uganda also counseled that a railroad be built to connect Lake Victoria to the sea at Mombasa. Following much debate in parliament, the decision was favorable. Construction of the line, dubbed the lunatic express by critics, began in 1896.

Mombasa was the beneficiary of British imperial aspirations. Railroad construction personnel, British managers and engineers plus laborers from India, inundated the town. A new bigger and deeper port was built at Kilindini on the opposite side of the island. Colonial officials, military personnel, eventually white settlers flocked to Kenya via Mombasa in the next half century. In the wake of Indian railroad laborers, thousands of other Indians also arrived in Mombasa. Soon the polyglot Arab, Swahili, and coastal Kenyan population became even more cosmopolitan with the inclusion of Europeans and Indians from many communities. On into the 20th century this influx continued. Gradually upcountry Kenyans too made their way to the coast. They came to work in the port and the factories. After independence they dominated the civil service and the police. In the post independence era, up country tribes solidified control of central government institutions and the military, but also staffed banks, shipping companies and burgeoning industries. Finally as tourism emerged as a viable industry in the sixties, there was an additional influx of personnel from various European countries there to cater to their fellow countrymen.

Because the groups differed racially and culturally, they also differed religiously. Islam arrived in Mombasa in the 9th century. The Swahili people, many from coastal tribes and, of course Arabs were followers of the Prophet. Several Asian communities were also Islamic, but Sikhs and Hindus were plentiful as well. Europeans and up-country Africans tended to be Christians. Nonetheless, the majority of people in Coast Province were Moslems. Consequently, virtually all of the politicians were as well.

In fact, it was this Islamic character of the coast that led the U.S. to re-establish a consulate at the coast. We moved the consulate from Zanzibar to Mombasa during the First World War to get away from the Germans, but it went back to Zanzibar in the twenties. A consulate was opened during WWII in order to purchase critical supplies, especially pyrethrum, a natural insecticide badly needed in the South Pacific. During the war a battalion of black American soldiers was posted to Mombasa. Their worldliness was an eye opener to the conservative society and buttressed the nascent independence movement with the idea that blacks could control their own destiny. That consulate was closed in the early fifties. I opened the current office in 1981. In the aftermath of hostage taking in Iran and the rise of militant Islamist movements throughout the Middle East, the U.S. signed an agreement with Kenya permitting military access to its port and airfields. Chief among my duties was to keep the pulse of the coast to ensure that the sense of welcome there tracked the good vibes emanating from the government in Nairobi. So far, I found that while a strident anti-Americanism reverberated among a few radicals, overall Islamic leaders and their communities displayed the broad mindedness characteristic of Mombasa over the centuries.

By my time in the 1980s the separate Mombasa communities lived more or less harmoniously side by side. They met and mixed in the market place, but kept somewhat apart otherwise. Tolerance was practiced as that was the centuries old legacy of the city. As U.S. consul, I did not automatically fit into any of the groups. So instead of being pigeon holed, I was welcomed everywhere. For example, I might meet with His Worship the Mayor and his council – mostly Swahilis from the coast in the morning, the (upcountry) Boran tribesman Provincial Commissioner at noon, a Kikuyu businessman in the afternoon and dine with an Ismaili group of South Asian Muslims in the evening.

The American community for which I had special responsibility was small. In addition to the consulate staff of five and their families, several dozen Peace Corps Volunteers were posted in Coast Province. About forty missionaries lived in the environs as well. Finally, there were small numbers of businessmen plus some Kenyan Americans, i.e. children of Kenyans born in the U.S. while their parents were studying there. Additionally, there were perhaps several dozen tourists in the province at any given time.

Second Thoughts

Florence was still shaken by the murder on her hall two days earlier. She had dodged inspector Oyugi's men yesterday who came to take witnesses out to the ship. She justified this to herself thinking that she really had not seen the man clearly. She thought briefly about absconding to Nairobi to be completely out of the affair, but did not have enough money for the bus. She had, however, compared notes about the murder with Maria. Maria averred that she had not seen any white man at the guest house, but she admitted to Florence that on the way to the toilet that night she had passed by Monica's door and found it ajar. She looked in and in the half light saw Monica lying completely nude, face up on the bed, apparently asleep. She tiptoed in and covered the girl, closing the door when retreating.

Florence said that Maria must tell this to Oyugi. About this time two police constables knocked on Maria's door. Finding the two women inside, they ordered them to accompany them to the station. "Oyugi wants to take a statement," they confided.

Inspector Oyugi told Florence that he was disappointed that she had not gone to the boat the day before. He threatened that if she did not cooperate with the investigation, she'd be tossed in jail herself. Chastised, she agreed to cooperate fully. Her statement, however, differed little from what she said earlier. She had only caught a glimpse of a white man, not enough she thought to indentify someone.

Dead end there, Oyugi thought, but Maria provided more useful information. Maria said she was in her room at the end of the hall on the night in question with her boy friend Charles. She had earlier sent James, who often sat outside with the askari, off to buy beer. He returned with five bottles of Tusker. She gave him one and she and Charles drank the others. She said after sex, they dozed off, but she was suddenly awakened by a scream. It sounded like a woman in distress. She said she stepped out on the little balcony of her room that overlooked the back courtyard, but heard no further noise. She returned to bed.

Then Maria told Oyugi of her later visit to the toilet, after midnight she swore, of seeing Monica's door open and of covering the woman and closing the door. "Was she alive?" he asked.

"I thought so at the time, but now I don't really know," Maria replied.

Oyugi mulled it over. Maria's statement again raised the time of death issue as had the coroner's report, but the key fact was not so much when, but what action resulted in the death. That's what constituted murder. Oyugi 's pressing need was to pin down a better identification of Tyrell. He hatched a plan. He would use Salim's identification from the ship, but strengthen it with a formal standard police line-up in Mombasa. In addition to the men, he would make sure that Florence was also there to point out Tyrell.

While he was interviewing the women, Tyrell was in a room in the back of the station. He had been escorted there that morning by Randle. Oyugi agreed that Randle could come back from noon to one and bring lunch for Tyrell. Meanwhile he had the police forensic team take blood and a sample of pubic hair for analysis. The chemist office earlier concluded that blood swabbed from Monica's body was type O, as was hers. Also semen in the used condom indicated type O. Oyugi knew that was not very conclusive as most people carried type O blood.

Oyugi saw that he had two objectives. One was to put Tyrell at the Taita Guest House crime scene. The other was to blow holes into his alibi of being at the Oceanic Hotel with his buddies. Oyugi knew that the corroborating statements would be viewed skeptically in court because they had been given by friends and were thus not impartial. He would concentrate on his primary task of linking Tyrell to the victim. Although he had a copy of Tyrell's statement taken on the carrier, he needed a detailed statement to him, the Kenyan investigator, from Tyrell about his evening in Mombasa.

That afternoon Oyugi and a police typist listened as Tyrell walked them through his day in Mombasa. It did not vary much from the information in the navy's version. Tyrell named his buddies, recounted their moves, and gave a good description of the Oceanic Hotel and its environs. Tyrell stated unequivocally that he wore jeans and a light brown collar shirt. Oyugi sought to pin down times quite precisely, especially the hours from 8 to 11. Tyrell was firm in his conviction that he spent those hours at the Oceanic in the company of friends and two Kenyan hookers. The statement was typed up and signed.

Prosecutor Mbai called to ask for an up-date. Oyugi briefed him and noted that he would like to arrange a standard identification line-up for Friday. Mbai said that was an excellent idea, but that to pass a veracity test, participants would have to be military looking white men. Where would he get them? Oyugi had no ready answer, perhaps I'll ask Randle to help he thought.

When Randle returned at five, Oyugi did bring up the topic of a line-up. "I will work on it," Randle promised.

Oyugi turned Tyrell over to agent Randle. "Bring him back tomorrow at nine," he ordered.

Randle called me that evening to brief me on the day's events. The new item was the line-up.

"Should we help out," I asked.

"We're in it deep already," he admitted, "if we don't provide sailors for the line-up, it will be a farce and Tyrell will be easily fingered."

"Good point," I agreed, "will the Ajax be around long enough to help out?"

"Yeah, I think I can persuade the navy to keep her here for a few more days."

"OK, let's do it. On another point, when does Tyrell need a lawyer? And who pays for it?"

"I am not sure on that point. Tyrell has not been charged yet."

"Certainly, that's coming, isn't it?" I interrupted.

"Yes, looks it. I'll ask about a lawyer."

Death in Mombasa

Monica Njere's body was buried in a pauper's grave in the Christian section of the city cemetery in Freretown. Since she was Kikuyu it was supposed that Monica was not Moslem. There were no mourners.

A plain wooden box sufficed for a coffin. However, a priest from the Anglican diocese of Mombasa recited the prayers of committal at graveside. It was a service, I learned later that the diocese performed regularly on behalf of those unclaimed.

Monica's mother had by this time been informed of her daughter's death. She was distraught as any mother would be, but was penurious and could not assemble the funds necessary either for a funeral or for travel to the coast in a timely fashion. Timeliness was always important with regard to the death in the stifling climate of the coast. Moslems were buried before dark on the day they died. Hindus were cremated within a day or so and Christians, whose remains were not sent up-country for burial in their home villages were usually consigned to the earth within a few days. The city had no western style mortuary facilities and the morgue at Coast General was usually full and not up to proper cooling standards.

As U.S. Consul I had, unfortunately, opportunities to view first-hand how the process of disposing of remains worked. Note that I had nothing to do with Monica Njere's case, but on several occasions in previous years when American citizens died, I assumed my consular responsibilities and assisted in local burials, which were not too difficult because family or friends made arrangements. My responsibility in those cases was to provide the consular certificate documenting the death of a U.S. citizen. However, on one occasion I had been asked by the husband of the deceased to witness her cremation. I agreed to the request. If asked, Hindu priests were willing to organize and supervise the cremation of non-Hindus at their temple. The shrouded body was placed on an outdoor pyre and burned. I admit to apprehension about the process, but found it to be a satisfying closure.

Most troublesome were deaths wherein families back home in the U.S. wanted remains returned. In these cases time was of the essence, not only for the climatic reasons, but also because families insisted that things happen fast. Unfortunately, the process could not begin until funds were in hand. The only agency in Mombasa authorized to package human remains for export was the city mortuary service, but it would not even begin construction of an export coffin until paid up-front. They made each coffin from scratch, welding a metal box together and then placing it inside a wooden crate. These were not sophisticated caskets, but they did meet international criteria for air transport. I once asked why they did not keep one or two already made on hand. The officer in charge admitted that was a good idea, but stated that he just did not have the funds to tie up in such an endeavor.

Meanwhile my task was to assemble the sheaf of documents – death certificate, sanitation certificate, bills of ladling, etc - required for shipment, finally bundling them all together under my U.S. consular seal affixed with red wax and ribbon. I was also charged with finding and inventorying personal affects and sending them onward to the family. I recall that the most onerous case in terms of documents had been that of a merchant seaman from the Lykes line. He had apparently fallen into the harbor drunk while the ship was in Majunga, Madagascar. He drowned. His body was fished from the sea, examined by authorities who declared him dead and gave a certificate to that effect. The master of the ship had the remains loaded aboard and departed Madagascar for Mombasa, the next port of call. His home office advised that the man's family wanted his body returned to Louisiana for burial. By the time the ship arrived in Mombasa, the crew was in a state of near mutiny. Their shipmate's body had been kept in the galley's walk in refrigerator. Consequently, spooked by this, the crew had refused to eat.

Now, it was difficult enough assembling all the documents required to ship a body out of Kenya, but we had to get this one into Kenya without much documentation. In discussing the case with the coroner Dr. Mohamed, he helpfully agreed that even though he could not issue a death certificate as such because a Madagascar one already existed, he could issue an official document confirming that the man was dead and authorizing the export of his remains from Kenya.

All deaths, of course, are sad, but I felt those that occurred unexpectedly in a far away land were particularly poignant. I was not friend or family, but had to act on their behalf in a time of sorrow. I was proud to do so and have always believed that this indispensable function of the consular service provides comfort and succor to families.

Special Branch

Special Branch chief Okoth had been intrigued by the information provided by Inspector Oyugi. Bile Hussein was a wanted radical. He was presumed to be plotting against President Moi and in the course of that laying the ground for radical Islamic operations. Through the embassy in Nairobi, American anti-terrorist analysts had asked for Kenyan's help in locating this individual and destroying his network. Not that the Special Branch needed that incentive, the threat against Kenya's leader was cause enough for action.

Okoth's staff had immediately looked up the phone number and found the address. It was indeed located in an apartment building home to several Somali families. The apartment in question was not leased by anyone named Hussein. However, the building itself had come to Special Branch attention on an earlier occasion. That made the information even more salient. Rather than raid the building, Okoth decided to put it under twenty four hour surveillance. He would also tap the phone.

Okoth bemoaned the fact that he had only sparse information about Islamic radicals. He tried to monitor preachers at various mosques through the use of informers; some paid, others operated under threat from the Special Branch of incarceration or some other sanction on account of their past deeds. Okoth knew, however, that information developed by such informers had to be carefully analyzed. He had more confidence in keeping his finger on the pulse of the

Moslem community via regular discussions with community leaders, including local Members of Parliament, none of whom were Somali. They, of course knew who he was, but they also knew that being straight with him was essential insurance in keeping their standing with State House in good order. Okoth also relied on a relationship he had cultivated with a Kenyan citizen of Somali origin – of which there were several tens of thousands – who headed a truckers' union. As with the MPs, this contact knew it was in his best interests, both personal and professional, to be forthright with the Special Branch. Through all of these contacts Okoth was aware of a growing fundamentalist Islamic sentiment. Much of it, in the Somali community in any case centering around the mysterious Bile Hussein.

The problem with Somalis was that the community was internally divided by clans, and there was great enmity among the various clans. These divisions that were the hallmark of political divisions in Somalia itself and the passions and prejudices moved easily across the border into Kenya. Okoth understood the dimensions of such divisions as they replicated the problems of tribalism in Kenya that pitted or allied various tribes in shifting alliances in the quest for national political power and the spoils that flowed there from. Therefore, Okoth knew that if his contact or informer was from the Hawiye clan, for example, his information regarding Darod or Digil clan members' views or activities must be treated as suspect, and vice versa.

AWOL

Two sullen looking men were seated in the hallway outside Senior Chief's office. When I got down to our suite, Catherine nodded back up the hallway at them. "Those are the guys who didn't show up in time. Now that he's got 'em they're gonna wish again that they made the departure. He reads the riot act to 'em for five minutes every hour. You can set your watch by it."

"So, two of the three have been found?" I asked.

"Yes, both of these more or less turned themselves in. The usual story; they were drunk and didn't know the time. One said he woke up in Kisumu and couldn't find his way back to the ship."

I looked skeptical. "Kisumu? That's five hundred miles away."

"Yeah, but not that Kisumu, Paul told Senior Chief that the local Kisumu is a neighborhood on the other side of the causeway where lots of Luo dockworkers live."

"Makes sense. What about the third? Any word on him?"

"Nope," she replied.

There were always a few stragglers who failed to get back to the ship before it departed. Like the two in the hallway, they usually turned up sheepishly a day or so later. Senior Chief would process them and send them up to Nairobi where the weekly naval supply flight from Diego Garcia to Sigonella would carry them to the brig in Italy for safe keeping. Eventually, they would be reunited with their ship to face disciplinary action there.

I expected that Randle would stop in after he deposited Tyrell at the police station that morning. Meanwhile I read the Nation's article about the investigation. It led with the statement that a sailor from the USS America was in custody, but then rehashed most of what had been published earlier. It did for the first time give the name of the deceased Monica Njere, but gave no more information about her.

Randle showed up a few minutes later.

"What are they going to do with him today?" I asked.

"Oyugi was not very forthcoming on that," Randle replied. "He said, he'd be checking out his story."

"Where do we stand on the line-up?"

"We're good on that score. Six men, more or less like Tyrell will be in tomorrow's line-up. I hope it doesn't get postponed because the Ajax has to leave on Saturday."

"I hope Tyrell will go with them."

"Not a chance," Randle fired back, "This Oyugi guy is going to milk this for all its worth. He's determined to get a conviction and he's not beyond underhanded tactics."

Taita Guest House

Randle was prescient, because that's exactly what Oyugi was up to even as we spoke.

Oyugi's driver pulled the car onto the broad dirt parking area under a mango tree just off Station Road. A shop faced the street with a sign stating "Housewares" hanging above. "Look," the inspector ordered Tyrell, "you must recognize this place."

"No," Tyrell responded, "I've never seen this place."

"Come on then, we'll refresh your memory." He led Tyrell around the corner to an open doorway that revealed a set of stairs leading upwards. "This is the Taita Guest House." The inspector went up first. At the first landing he turned around and scrutinized his man, but Tyrell displayed no outward signs of nervousness. Oyugi stepped down the hall and paused at the second door on the left. "Know where you are now?" He queried.

Again, Tyrell just said, "no, I've never been here."

They went into the room. It hadn't been touched, just as the police ordered, but the sparse furnishings remained. The metal framed bed with bare metal springs sat in the middle of the room, the small table beside it. Nothing more. Oyugi looked around slowly and let Tyrell do the same. "This is where you strangled her, isn't it? It's okay, you can admit it now and it will be all over. No more interrogation. With a good lawyer, you'll go back to the navy in no time. We Kenyans don't want to lock up American friends." Oyugi paused. "Show me how you did it. She was a big girl, was she not doing what you wanted? These whores get uppity and need a blow or two to straighten 'em out. So you hit her first, like this," he punched out with his right hand, "then she screamed and fought back. So you got mad. She was drunk, to shut her up, you grabbed her throat and squeezed. Before you knew it, it was over. You panicked and ran out. Isn't that so?

Tyrell remained silent. Oyugi pressed," But folks here saw you: the taxi driver, the watchman and the man upstairs. Other whores saw you too. I know you're guilty and can prove it. Save me the effort and admit your error. The law will go easy on you. She was just a whore. She won't be missed."

Tyrell was cowed, even stunned by Oyugi's outburst. Still, he managed to repeat, "I've never been here. I did not kill anyone." They exchanged hard looks. Neither saw a weakness in the other. But the inspector was not yet finished. "OK," he conceded graciously, "you weren't here. Then let's go."

They shuffled back into the hallway. Standing there to the left alongside a police constable were Florence and Maria. Oyugi did not say a word to them, but pulled Tyrell away towards the stair well.

Outside, Oyugi pointed out the taxi stand. "Do you remember the color of the car?" He asked, "You're a smoker. Where is your lighter?"

Tyrell had heard that question before. He had denied having a lighter and decided it best to keep quiet.

Oyugi smirked silently to himself as he loaded Tyrell into the car for the return trip to the station. I hope she got a good look at him.

Tyrell recounted the morning's trip to agent Randle over lunch. Randle brought him a hamburger with all the fixings from Fontana just down the street. "When do I get out of here?" Tyrell asked. "These guys are serious and it's getting scary."

"I won't lie to you bub," Randle replied, "You're in deep kimchi. I don't at all like the crime scene visit he did to you this morning. The Kenyans want a perp and you're the only guy they got. Steel up, we've got a good team here working for you; even the ambassador is using his influence. "

That afternoon Oyugi again toured Tyrell around, but this time to places he claimed to have visited. Tyrell affirmed that he'd been at the

Castle Hotel. He recognized the Oceanic as well and told Oyugi, who had never been there, how to get to the pool or to go down to the casino. Oyugi seemed content with the walk through and did not ask many questions.

Meanwhile back in my office, Randle braced me with the news of the visit to Taita Guest House.

"How damaging is this?" I queried, "Tyrell did not confess to anything did he?"

"No, "Randle said, "but it stinks all the same. Oyugi's got something up his sleeve." He continued, "Again we are faced with a ship movement issue. The Ajax leaves Saturday. I've told Oyugi that Tyrell should be on it."

"And his reply?"

"Only a snide smile."

The Line Up

Friday morning at the police station, Oyugi sat in his office reviewing the committal bundle of documents that he would file with the high court later that day. All that was missing was a confession and further good identification. He expected that the identity line-up scheduled for the next hour would provide more of what he wanted. Not for nothing he mused confident that Florence got a good look at Tyrell only yesterday. Too bad that she had coincidently been there when he led Tyrell around.

Randle arrived shortly before ten with the six volunteers for the line-up. All were dressed, as Tyrell would be, in jeans and a white tee shirt. It was a pretty simple event the seven men stood against a wall with the light in their face and a number at their feet. The witnesses – Salim, James, Samuel and Florence – were brought in and given about five minutes to look at the men. Randle, Oyugi and several police officials watched or ran it.

Afterwards, Samuel and James both said they could not identify anyone. Salim, who had picked out Tyrell onboard, choose one of the

Ajax men this time. Florence too, despite Oyugi's best effort, identified another of the Ajax men as the culprit.

Randle gave a great sigh of relief. "So, that's it?" He asked Oyugi, "is he free to go?"

"No," Inspector Oyugi replied, "Only a setback. I am filing committal documents this hour. I'll have an arrest warrant soon afterwards. I will formally arrest this man. Kenya will take custody of him and he'll be bound over for trial."

Randle was flabbergasted, "Inspector, you have no case. This man did not do it. He has not been identified by witnesses. His alibi is airtight. Perhaps some sailor from the America did murder the girl, but it simply was not this man."

"We'll see," Oyugi responded, "that's why we have courts."

Hiring a Lawyer

Randle was visibly flustered when he told me about Oyugi's stubborn intent to proceed. He saw in it clear evidence that Tyrell was being railroaded. However, we did not see any options. We had decided to go down the cooperation track and this was where it led. I reaffirmed that under the applicable agreement governing the status of U.S. military forces in Kenya, the Kenyan government did have jurisdiction and could arrest Tyrell for murder. We agreed that it was time for a good lawyer.

"How would that work?" I asked. I sketched out my limitations. "Normally, all I can do as consul is provide arrested Americans with a list of local lawyers. I am not authorized to hire or pay for a lawyer for a citizen in distress, but can assist with communications back and forth to family and friends. I am also able to visit citizens in jail or prison in order to keep up contact and to ensure that they are fairly treated. I have also attended hearings and trials to show the flag and put authorities on notice that the U.S. is watching. But back to Tyrell, it doesn't seem that he has the resources to hire a lawyer. Would the Navy help?"

"I hope so, XO Miller who got him into this mess ought to foot the bill personally," Randle groused. "There is a mechanism through the JAG office that the navy can use to help. I know they've been tracking developments here. I'll press on the need for a defense lawyer with them."

"Good, I will also underline that need in my cable."

I passed the information onto DCM Hawkins, advising that a reporting cable stressing the need for a good lawyer would be on the wires soon. I suggested that once the arrest was made it would be good for the ambassador to review the issue with the Attorney General. In my opinion Kenya needed to be very clear on our view that the conviction of an innocent man for political purposes was intolerable.

"Calm down," Dan told me, "rest assured that the ambassador will make the right noises here. I don't think, however, that the powers-that-be are as willing to railroad him as you think. But they do have the press screaming at them and need to find a way through."

"Come on," I retorted, "you know that they are perfectly capable of cold blooded murder when it's politically expedient. They need to know that the price for doing in an American will be very high."

"OK, OK, your point is made. I think that we're on the same page. You sit tight on the situation there and we'll handle the politics up here."

I hung up hoping that I hadn't blotted my copybook with my bosses, but they needed an unvarnished view of what I saw happening.

I carefully drafted my cable, but held back on sending it until Randle confirmed that an arrest warrant had been served. Tyrell was in a cell at the central police station.

Searching for a Suspect

The Ajax sailed at dawn. The U.S. Navy presence in Mombasa was down to Senior Chief Woodley, NIS agent Randle, Seaman First Class Jim Tyrell (in jail) and the not yet located sailor whose name was Charles Pope. It was a Saturday. Although I normally played golf in the morning, the Tyrell affair weighed heavily on my mind and there were some arrangements to make.

I met with Senior Chief and Randle at the consulate. Senior Chief insisted that, now free from the exigencies of the port visit, he take over the care and feeding of the jailed seaman. Randle conceded. He noted that since the "investigation" of this event was over that he would soon have to leave. He reported he had been in touch by phone with Navy JAG personnel in Washington. He was certain they would provide funds for a lawyer and would probably send a case manager out to Mombasa the next week to hire one.

We reviewed the process for visiting Tyrell. The police allowed only one visit a day to the holding cell at the station. The visitor was allowed to bring food. Senior Chief said he would take him a good meal every day at noon, starting in an hour.

The two Navy men compared notes on how to find Charles Pope. As mentioned earlier, normally these guys showed up of their own accord, but there had been no word from Pope. Randle had some scoop on Pope. He summarized a report from the ship. Pope was described as being five feet five inches tall; 150 pounds, brown hair, hairy arms, a light mustache; smokes Marlboros, has a tattoo on left forearm; has A negative blood. He was last seen wearing jeans and a white striped short sleeved shirt. His last reported presence was at the Castle Hotel during the evening of 8 April. Randle noted that Pope was also ashore on the night of the murder, but friends swore he was in their company the whole time. Still, Randle wondered, why was he on the lam?

Senior Chief said he had asked a contact at the airport to check departing passenger lists, but no name turned up. Of course, there were many other ways to leave town. I suggested a canvass of cheap hotels in town and on the beaches north and south. We hatched a plan of phoning around as well as visiting a few of the more likely spots. Two beach facilities in particular, one north towards Kilifi and another on the south coast near Tiwi catered to young low budget travelers such as Peace Corps Volunteers and overlanders (twenty something folks traversing Africa in big trucks).

I offered to go north to the Sun and Sand. I went home, collected the family and promised them lunch and a swim. We turned right onto the main north road leaving the residential area of Nyali with its graceful red tile roofed houses, palm trees, and colorful red, white, orange and purple bougainvillea draped over walls. The Bamburi cement quarries gaped to the left. They were rather immense holes where fossilized coral had been dug up and processed into cement. Interestingly a Swiss scientist had begun a – so far – successful project to reclaim the quarry pits by a process of creating a new ecology from zero. He planted casuarina pines, added caterpillars to digest the needles, then spiders to control the caterpillars, then wasps and birds to control the spiders, etc. As everything got out of balance a new species was introduced to counteract it. Ultimately antelope, hippos, tilapia fish and crocodile farms joined the system. The reclamation project won praise for innovation.

Past Bamburi the rural coast reasserted itself. It was a timeless place of small mud houses surrounded by subsistence crops, mango and cashew trees. Drying wash hung on the fences. Children tumbled about; other inhabitants went about their daily business or sat serenely in their bare earth yards.

Just before crossing the bridge at Mtwapa Creek, I had to slow down and swerve around the bent metal spikes of a police barricade near the front entrance to Shemu la Tewa prison. Seeing my diplomatic plates the constables manning the check point waved us through. Generally, any one white or driving a nice car was waved through. The police harassed drivers of local minibus taxis, called matatus, and truckers for small bribes.

After the bridge was the small commercial center of Mtwapa. The road there was thronged with walkers on this market day. On an acre or so of little sheds and stands vendors sold fruit – mangos, pineapples, oranges, papayas and much more - and produce of all varieties. There were fish mongers and local butcheries, live chickens and goats. Bread, dried goods including rice, flour, sugar, were displayed as were various spices and cooking oils. Other sections of the market sported clothes and shoes – new and used, lengths of colorful cotton fabrics so prized by local women, house wares, pots and pans, and cassette tapes of the latest music - usually pirated. Several stands sold medicines and home remedies for maladies and others magic potions. Truly there was something there for everyone. And if you weren't buying, then the prospects for conversation, catching up with neighbors and the latest news were intriguing.

We did not stop, but probably would on the way home to get a fresh pineapple. Beyond the market, a large sisal plantation appeared. Fiber from the prickly fleshy leaves was thrashed out and turned into twine and rope. Grown and processed locally, sisal was a rare success in bringing a modern, i.e. money making, crop to the coast. A better money maker was tourism and I soon saw the turn off to the Sun and Sand Hotel.

We parked in a sandy area defined by white painted trunks of palm trees lying on the ground just behind the main structure. The boys whooped with joy, jumped out of the car and headed for the beach. Carol dutifully followed. I said I would be along in a minute and turned towards the building. A line of small ocean front bungalows stretched up and down the beach, but I followed a sign that said "Reception" to a small alcove that segued into a large restaurant area topped with a palm frond thatched roof. It was open on three sides to the ocean.

"Jambo, bwana, karibu" I was greeted politely by a young man at the desk. He appeared to be a Giriama man from the region. He was dressed in a kanzu, an ankle length dress-like wrap that coastal men typically wore.

I explained that my family and I were there for lunch and a swim. He nodded and advised that lunch would be their famous curry buffet which would be available beginning at noon. The day use charge for the premises and pool would be twenty shillings each for the two adults. I paid the fee and added that I was the American consul from Mombasa and was also searching for an American sailor who had gone missing.

"Do you have any young American men staying here?"

He thought for a minute. "Ndio, there is one. I think he is American Peace Corps." He pronounced corps "corpse" in the typical Kenyan fashion. Consulting the register, he added, "His name is Jerry Lee. He and his girlfriend are in banda 12." He pointed.

"Asante sana, that's very helpful." I thanked him.

I walked out to the beach where Carol was sunning while the boys built a castle in the sand. "I have something to check out. I don't think it's him, but I'll be back in a few minutes, then we can do lunch. Will the boys be okay?"

"They'll be fine," she smiled and squinted up at me. "Don't be too long."

I cut through the lawn to the path running in front of the bandas. It was a pretty place, well landscaped. The hotel was cheap, relatively speaking, because it was old. The establishment dated even from the forties. It had been modernized a bit over the years, but had none of the fanciness – high end restaurants, discos and casinos - of the newer and much larger resort establishments. The Sun and Sand's clientele too tended to be local, mostly long term resident expats from up-country. There did not seem to be anyone at banda 12, I said "hodi, hodi,' but no one answered. A towel was hanging on an outside line. I saw a woman on the beach in front of the banda. Wearing a blue bikini, a floppy hat and sunglasses, she looked up from her book as I approached.

"Mr. Nichols?" she queried.

"Yes," I replied a bit surprised.

She removed her sun glasses. "It's me, Rachel. Rachel Berger from Wundanyi."

"Of course," I caught myself. She's the Peace Corps teacher whose school I visited a couple of months back. "Rachel, I did not expect to see you here. I was looking for a guy named Jerry Lee."

"Well," she pointed out to the ocean, "that's him out there snorkeling. Why are you looking for him?"

"I'm not really. I am looking for a missing sailor and was checking out this hotel. The clerk said there was a young American man here named Jerry Lee. I am really looking for a guy named Charles Pope. "

"Oh, "she nodded "there were some sailors around early in the week, but they've gone. Jerry is Peace Corps too. He drills wells up near Maralal." She waved at the swimmer and motioned for him to come in. "I'll introduce you."

The man sat in the shallows and removed his fins, then sauntered up the sand. He was a nice looking guy, fit, but his lighter torso contrasted with sun darkened face, arms and legs, evidence of outside work. "Jerry," I stuck out my hand, "Cliff Nichols, I'm the consul from Mombasa."

"Pleased to meet ya," he grinned. "What's up?"

I repeated what I had told Rachel. I was looking for a missing sailor and the clerk had given me his name as an American man staying there.

"Clearly, you are not my man. Sorry to have bothered you, but have you met any wandering sailors?

Rachel said, "there was a bunch of 'em here last Tuesday, maybe a dozen or more. They came out for the day, ate lunch and drank a lot of beer. I kept fending them off, but they were young and lonely and wanted to talk to a girl. I was flattered, but relieved when they finally left."

"Yeah," Jerry agreed, "It was a crazy day. They kept buying beer. I don't remember many names, but Charles doesn't ring a bell. It's been quiet around here since then. Is this linked to the murder we've been reading about?"

"No," I replied, "the police have arrested another sailor for that. Pope didn't get back to the ship in time for sailing. Right now he is just AWOL – absent without leave, but If he does not turn up soon, he will be classified as a deserter." Shifting the topic, pointing down the beach, "my wife Carol and the boys are playing on the beach there. We're gonna have lunch. Stop by and say hi."

"Glad too," they chorused.

Dead end here I thought as I ambled back to the family, but worth checking out.

Tiwi Beach

On Sunday morning, Senior Chief with Randle in tow made a similar trip to the south coast. Such a trip always started with the hustle and bustle of the Likoni ferry. It's a big open ferry that takes five lines of vehicles and several hundred passengers. It is noisy and smelly, always kind of festive and my kids loved it. Once underway, crossing the Kilindini channel took about ten minutes.

The channel is the deep body of water that leads into the spacious inner harbor. There had been talk over the years of bridging or tunneling, but the cost of either seemed to outweigh the benefit. The ferry worked fine; besides already on the books was planning for a new road from the airport on the mainland around the back side of the harbor to the south coast.

None of that helped the navy team, but on Sunday the ferry was not crowded. Their objective, the camp ground at Tiwi was not far away. At the sign posted turn off a couple of little commercial establishments called hotelis in Swahili where one could get tea, beer or a simple meal sat on the corners of the main road. Randle noted with amusement that one called itself Alabama Central.

The camp ground was a business run by a retired British civil servant from the colonial era. His old style beach house sat at one end of the property. He probably did not make much money, but the camping areas consisted of several hundred yards of wonderful beach front, backed by shade trees. Two bath houses provided water and toilets, picnic tables and fire rings were scattered about. The final touch was a small duka that sold beer, soda, bread, and some other basics, such as toilet paper, a commodity only required by wazungu. The camp site drew some intrepid expatriate resident families that loved (or could only afford) to camp, but it was also a regular destination for overland groups. Those expeditions pulled together a dozen to twenty folks and carted them around Africa. Almost all participants were young and looking for adventure. Some were mid-way on a trek from London to Cape Town, others on inexpensive camping tours through Kenya's famous game parks.

As they pulled in, Senior Chief noted several dozen small tents pitched near two big overland trucks plus several other individual camps. The trucks were true monsters, former British military vehicles with all wheel drive. They were fitted out with comfortable seats in the truck bed and the tarpaulin canopy sides rolled up so passengers could watch Africa roll by. One even had a trailer for extra gear.

Their vehicle drew little attention. The navy men parked under a tree and began to walk around. Soon they were chatting with a sun blasted long haired hippie, a Brit, who identified himself as the driver mechanic for one of the big rigs.

"Just down from London," he stated, "It was a hell of a trip. Too much mud in the Congo. We're a couple of weeks behind schedule, but we have to rest... and I'm waiting on money to buy new shocks. We're not going anywhere for a while. "

Senior Chief said he represented the U.S. Navy and was looking for a missing man.

"That would be Chuck," the mechanic observed. "He's shacked up with Evelyn. I saw them go down to the beach a while back."

Thanking the man, they hurried off. They found the couple sitting under a palm tree at the sand's edge. The man looked up, "oh, no" and stood up. Senior Chief asked, "Are you Charles Pope?"

The man replied, "If I said no, would you leave me alone?"

"No," Randle replied, "we've got you. You are AWOL from the USS America. You may come with us voluntarily, or you can be arrested, your choice."

"I'll go," he said looking forlornly at Evelyn. She was an attractive young lady. Randle told me that she filled her little bikini up in all the right places. She cried a bit, but there was not much of a scene. The navy men allowed them a private good bye. In the car on the way back, Chuck said,"Hey guys, can I catch a break? You saw what a wonderful woman she was. I will go with you now, but I told her I'll be back. I'll split again, if I have to."

Back at the consulate, Randle pulled Pope's file. He appeared to be an average sailor. There were no blemishes on his record, but no commendations either. Even though the type A negative blood and the statements by Pope's buddies provided evidence that he was not involved in the murder, his stature, coloring and Marlboros fit the muddled descriptions provided by the witnesses. Randle asked Pope to explain his whereabouts on the night in question. As best he could remember, Pope recalled drinking at the Castle Hotel terrace, followed by dinner at some fancy upstairs restaurant called Hunter's something, more drinking in a nearby club, then back to the ship. It all tracked the friends' statements.

"We've just got a love sick AWOL," he told me, "not a murderer."

Navy Lawyer

On Tuesday morning, Senior Chief escorted Lt. Commander Tom Bonham in to meet me. Bonham was a navy lawyer from JAG corps headquarters in Crystal City, Virginia, just next to the Pentagon. Bonham looked like a lawyer rather than a naval officer. He was a little pudgy, of medium build, dark curly hair and wore dark rimmed glasses. Of course, he carried a brief case. He later told me he had done NROTC at Chapel Hill, then law school on the navy's dime at UVA in Charlottesville.

After introductions he began with a compliment. "Admiral Casey, my boss, sends his greetings and commendations for the professional manner that you've handled this case. Your reporting has been most helpful and one of the main reasons why I am here. " He then got down to the priority. "I need to hire a defense attorney as soon as possible. I need a man with criminal defense experience, who is well known and who has a good reputation. I will have to meet with him and check references."

"Sounds like a job," I agreed. "Here's our list of local lawyers. It is up to date. Additionally, I have asked around. Two possibilities seem viable. First is Fernando da Souza. He's a Goan, that means his family was originally from India, but he is a Kenyan citizen. He's defended several infamous cases over the past years and he certainly knows his way around the local court system. Another choice might be George Murunga. He's younger, less experienced, but is a black African, a Kikuyu. That might be an asset in a case that already has racial overtones."

"I know both men pleasantly. Da Souza is a flamboyant guy, a fixture in Asian society circles. In addition to his law practice, he is a real estate mogul involved especially in hotel deals. Muranga is a member of the Mombasa Rotary Club, I belong to the Kilindini Rotary Club, but there is some flow back and forth. He's well liked and seems destined for a solid career." I concluded, "If neither of these men is acceptable, I think we ought to look at someone from Nairobi."

"I'll get right on it," Bonham said.

Later that afternoon, Bonham checked back in with me. He found a strong contrast between the two prospects. Da Souza was outspoken, but confident that from what little he knew about the Tyrell case from the papers, the government did not have much. He had laid out for discussion several cases he defended and won. Bonham admitted to being impressed with his experience. Muranga was cautious and apprehensive about all the media attention to the case. However, he noted that Kenyan courts did not employ juries as such. Instead the presiding judge decided and most had shown themselves able to rise above public opinion.

Bonham said he was inclined to go with the more experienced da Souza, but wanted to discuss the racial issue again with me. I noted that it was all tied back to the Bellinger case several years earlier. An American sailor off the USS La Salle admitted to being drunk and beating a prostitute. She later died and he was tried and convicted of manslaughter. There was lots of press attention to the case. Bellinger's mother came to the trial and pleaded for her son. The prostitute was transformed – as was being done for Monica as well - into a fallen angel. In the end the court presided over by an English judge, seconded to the Kenyan bar, found the sailor guilty. However, instead of imposing prison time, he turned him loose with a minimal fine. The public was outraged. They saw it as a throwback to colonial times and free license for whites to kill Africans. The US Navy angle also played with accusations that the U.S. government threatened to withhold aid if the man was not freed.

"My concern now," I told Bonham, "is that an Asian defense lawyer – Asians are not Kenya's most beloved citizens - an Asian lawyer with a white navy client will evoke too much baggage from the past. I know that Tyrell is not getting a fair shake from the police or the media now because of that case. Prior to hiring da Souza, you ought to get his view on this angle."

"Yep," Bonham agreed, "I'll do that."

State House Nairobi

In the small conference room at State House Nairobi, Cheruyiot assembled the same ministerial players.

Nodding at the police commissioner, he said, "Okay Phillip, you've arrested the American sailor, what next?"

Before he could answer Attorney General Makupa interjected, "he'll be brought before a court for charging and then be bound over for trial."

"And how long will all that take?" asked the Foreign Minister.

"Robert, you're a lawyer. You know it usually takes several months," the AG replied.

"Well, in this instance," the minister responded, "we'll have to be faster. This case is already a thorn in relations with the U.S. Articles have appeared in the U.S. press accusing Kenya of kangaroo justice. Our legal system gets enough criticism from human rights organizations, including our own. These are troubles we don't need. If there is still time to drop the charges, we should do so."

"No Robert," Cheruyiot stated, "we shouldn't. We need to see this through. Our system needs to prevail. This is an opportunity to show how justice works. If he is guilty, he'll hang, if not he'll be released. The facts will speak."

"Well," Robert conceded, "make it fair and do it quickly."

"I agree. We can push the case forward on the calendar, provided the defense does not object." The AG declared, "unlike the last US Navy murder case, having the right Kenyan judge on the bench will be important. I will speak quietly to the Chief Justice to ensure that a good man is assigned. "

"Agreed," Cheruyiot smiled.

The Murder Statute

Section 202 of the Penal Code of Kenya: (1) Any person who by an unlawful act or omission causes the death of another person is guilty of the felony called manslaughter. (2) An unlawful omission is an omission amounting to culpable negligence to discharge a duty tending to the preservation of life or health, whether such omission is or is not accompanied by an intention to cause death or bodily harm.

Section 203: Any person of malice aforethought causes the death of another person by an unlawful act of omission is guilty of murder.

Section 204: Any person convicted of murder shall be sentenced to death.

I went over to the Central Police Station at noon along with Senior Chief Woodley. It was my first face-to-face meeting with Tyrell, but I felt I had known him for a while. Senior Chief was able to visit him while in police custody, but once he was transferred to the prison only family, his lawyer or me, in my capacity as U.S. consul would be able to visit him. I found Tyrell pretty much as described by Randle and others. He was a modest carefully spoken man, but clearly bewildered by the situation. Woodley brought a meal of roast chicken, potatoes and a salad, which Tyrell relished. We did not tell him that might be the last good food he'd get for a while. While he ate, we made small talk about football in western Pennsylvania; Joe Namath being from Beaver Falls near Tyrell's home town in New Castle.

I told him that a navy lawyer had arrived and was in the process of hiring a local defense lawyer for him.

"So, it's not over?" he asked hopefully.

"No, the case will go to trial. The Kenyan police are intent on making a show. You will probably be formally charged this afternoon."

James Mason Tyrell was brought before the criminal court in Mombasa and formally charged with murder under section 203 of the criminal code of Kenya. It was a perfunctory proceeding which Bonham and I observed. Bonham took copious notes, he even sketched the chamber. Tyrell was not required to speak or plea. In binding Tyrell over for trial before the magistrate's court, the document did provide for a plea of guilty to manslaughter. That was the first we had heard that the prosecution might want to deal. However, since murder was a capital offense, no bail was allowed. Tyrell was to be transferred to Shemu la Tewa prison pending trial.

Obviously tipped off as to the afternoon's proceedings, the press were present. A photographer managed a shot while Tyrell was being led back to a police van. It was front page news the next day under the caption, "Murderer."

Given the way things were moving, Bonham decided to engage da Souza. Da Souza went right to work, reviewing the committal documents that showed the basis for the charges of murder and the evidence against Tyrell. He phoned me at mid-day," I'm aghast, we need to meet, but let's find a neutral site. I don't want to be seen at your office and it would be good if you avoided mine. Let's meet in the men's bar at the chini club at 3:00. There won't be anyone there at that hour and we can have a private chat."

I walked into the Mombasa Club just before three. It was a stately old white building that had been in existence for almost a hundred years. Created as a haven for colonial officials and English settlers and adventurers, it served that clientele for decades. However, since independence the club admitted the full range of Kenyans adding Asians, Swahilis, Arabs and the full panoply of black Kenyans. Even so, it remained a hidebound, occasionally snooty place, still tied to the traditions of the past. For example, there was a dress code and women were only recently admitted as members; previously they could only enter the premises with a man. The men's' bar remained a redoubt, exempt from feminine presence. That mystic of privilege aside, it was just a bar, albeit a nice one. It had lots of wood, attentive staff and a magnificent view through the swaying palm trees of the old harbor.

Two older men were playing snooker, but otherwise the bar was deserted. I ordered a fresh lime from the waiter clad in a white kanzu and settled down at a small table. Fernando soon joined me.

"Why the secrecy?" I asked.

"Well, given the profile of the case," he replied, "I think it best to minimize links to the U.S. diplomatic presence in Kenya, lest we give the impression that undue pressure is being applied."

"Okay," I noted, "but there is great interest in the case by my government and especially by the navy. After all, the navy is footing your bill. Bonham will want to stay very much in the picture."

"No problem there" Fernando confirmed, "maybe I am over reacting, but let's be prudent for the time being. Later, I will want you visibly present at the trial."

"Good. So, why are you aghast?"

"I thought from reading the newspapers that the government had no case, but having read the committal documents, I know they don't. They have no valid identification and the man's alibi is solid. So the issue is why are they going to trial? The answer must be that the government feels it must. It must protect a dead Kenyan girl. It must find a scapegoat and to do that I fear that it means to convict Tyrell no matter what."

"So, what's your counter tactic?"

"We need a two-fold strategy. First, I will shoot holes in the prosecution's case. But I have to do that without making it look like I am belittling or denigrating the police officers involved. As part of that I need to unequivocally verify Tyrell's alibi. Secondly, if I may be bold, your ambassador needs to ensure that the puppet masters in Nairobi understand that there will be consequences – as I hope there would be – if Tyrell is railroaded." He added hastily," I do not want to know what's going on at that level, but I wanted to tell you that it should be done."

"All right, thanks. I can assure you that the ambassador is already engaged at the ministerial level on this case along the lines you suggested. I am sure he will stay the course. Regarding the case, is there anything I can do?"

"Yes," Fernando agreed, "Tyrell's account of his time ashore was corroborated by five ships mates. I have their statements as recorded by agents on board the USS America. I agree they are convincing and exculpatory, but those statements will not be accepted into evidence by a Kenyan court. Thus, we need for the five to come to Mombasa and make statements to the Kenyan Police. Would that be possible?"

"I'll see what I can do," I promised.

Before we parted, da Souza said he would visit Tyrell the next day at the prison in order to thoroughly vet the alibi statement. He added, "Foreigners have a tough time in Shemu la Tewa, not from bad treatment, but from miserable, hot conditions. I had an Englishman there for several months last year and he almost died from despair. Do what you can to keep his spirits up."

Back in the office, I passed the task on to Bonham. He groaned, "Who knows where the America is now and how the men would get to Mombasa – even if they were authorized?" But he agreed it was a good idea. "I'll get on it."

I then called Hawkins to fill him in on da Souza's concerns and requests. "You gave him the right answer on contacts here," Hawkins said. "We'll take care of them. Bringing the navy men back will be the navy's call. Too bad statements were not taken when the ship was in port. Whatever, that's water over the dam. Rest easy that the embassy will help as necessary."

Recriminations

Bile carefully laid the morning paper on the stack on the small table near the door. He had been following the saga closely and was relieved that an American had finally been charged in the murder. "I hope he hangs," the Somali muttered to himself. "The blundering imperialists deserve it."

Bile's current hideaway was deep in the bowels of Changamwe, the vast semi-slum that sprawled between the port and the airport. People of many tribes Luos, Kambas, Digos,Taitas and, of course Somalis scratched out a livelihood or found a hovel or dilapidated apartment in the area. It was the sort of place where police presence was minimal and where questions weren't asked. Yet, Bile knew he was a wanted man. He moved his abode regularly and limited contacts to his most trusted disciples.

Glancing again at the newspaper, he felt nothing but repugnance for the Kikuyu prostitute, even though he recognized that she was a victim, both of imperial system he was dedicated to overthrow – what society permits its women to sell their bodies? - as well as of his own struggle. She had, he remembered, passed a message to him from a leader of the New Kikuyu Association, an outlawed upcountry group that was also interested in eradicating President Moi. However, even the existence of that contact grated upon him. Bile knew that Kikuyu radicals simply wanted to dispossess the Kalinjin leadership. They might talk revolution, but they really just wanted regime change. Even so, he reflected, the common goal of disruption, destruction and chaos in Kenya would favor strengthening the authority, purpose and growth of Islam. For the time being, he resolved, he would maintain sporadic communication with the New Kikuyu contact.

Bile correctly suspected that authorities had stumbled upon some link between the dead girl and Siad's apartment - sloppy work by the Kikuyus. He trusted the situation was fixed. He smirked, the Special Branch oafs had been quickly spotted, but the communications drop site had been compromised and he would never be able to use it or Siad again. Insha'allah. God wills it.

Perhaps, he thought, it was time again to retreat to Mogadishu. He needed to recharge, to recommit, to find more financing and to plan. Contact there with likeminded Imans and others would pay dividends in years to come. Our struggle, he reminded himself, can be a long one.

Shemu la Tewa Prison

A day or so later Bonham told me that the America had agreed to send Tyrell's buddies back to Mombasa in order to give statements.

The five would be flown by the carrier's long distance supply aircraft called a COD to Muscat. (Apparently the USS America battle group was somewhere in the Arabian Gulf.) From there they could, in fact, catch a weekly Kenya Airways flight to Nairobi.

I had earlier told Bonham of my talk with da Souza and our agreement to maintain a low profile. I assured him that this would not impair his contacts with the lawyer. "So," I asked, "what's da Souza up to? Is there a date for the trial?"

"Good news on that account. Da Souza says that the prosecutor appeared receptive to a request for a speedy trial. Maybe even in a month or so."

Sebastian carefully parked in one of the four spaces next to the guard booth guarding the arch way entrance of the prison. He hustled around to open the door for me. The crushed coral crunched under foot. The outside of the prison was not unattractive. It was a long wall of aged coral block. Mangos, palms and frangi pangi trees provided shade and evidence that the edifice had been there for years. The fragrance of the flowers cast their mellow tropic scent into the light breeze. The guard booth was painted Kenyan flag colors – red, green and black. The man on duty looked at my consular card and directed me through the open arch way to the office block inside. I was to see "Bwana Welfare."

I followed down a hall, saw a sign that said "welfare" and knocked on the half open door. "Hodi, hodi," I queried. "Karibu, come in" was the reply. The middle aged man sitting behind the desk looked up as I entered. Then he stood. He wore a well worn guard's uniform. He smiled. We shook hands and he introduced himself as James Minani, but he said just to call him Bwana Welfare because that's what he did. His job was to see to the well being of the prisoners and remands. He was the contact for families, lawyers and other visitors such as myself. He had been told that the U.S. consul would be coming to see the new white man in the remand section. He explained the rules. One visit a week. I would need to sign in and out with him. He'd escort the prisoner to a room where we could talk for a half hour or so. I could give the man cigarettes, a book or a little money, but no food or drink. Mail had to be censored both in and out. He'd do that. I asked about medicine, noting that wazungu weren't immune to malaria, and that Tyrell needed his pills. Bwana Welfare said that all medicines had to be left with him. In turn he would pass them to the nurse who would supervise daily administration. "Okay," I had to agree.

Bwana Welfare led me back to the inner courtyard and then into an adjacent hallway. He ushered me into a small room containing a table and several wooden chairs. There was a small barred window high in the wall. It was hot. "Wait here," he counseled, "I'll bring your man."

He returned shortly with Tyrell. He said, "a guard is posted at the end of the hall. Let him know when you are finished." Tyrell looked pale. He managed a smile and said,"am I glad to see you."

"Hello, Jim," I replied and gave him a hug. He was wearing prison garb – baggy white shorts and a worn white tee shirt. I asked him how things were.

"Pretty bad," he admitted. "It's hot and crowded and noisy. I'm locked in a big room with about twenty other guys. We have some mattresses that we unfold at night and sleep on the floor. The toilets stink and there really isn't a shower, just a tap to wash under. I am the only white guy there so they are always poking fun at me. Luckily I don't understand most of what they're saying. Food is terrible. Some sort of gruel for breakfast with a piece of bread, then what they call ugali and a sauce of some sort for dinner just before dark. I haven't got the shits yet," he confided, "but I'm sure they'll come."

"Do you get outside at all?" I asked.

"Yeah, we do. There is a court yard we go to. There is a bit more room there, some shade and a few benches. A guard said that because we are remand prisoners, we are not allowed to work or to have better cells. We're just supposed to hang out until we get a trial. Some of the guys," he noted with a shrug, "have been in remand for over a year. I don't think I could take that."

I updated him on events. He said he had met with da Souza. "I like him," he said, "he seems to know what he's doing."

"Yes," I agreed, "he does." I told him that the navy was pulling out all the stops. His shipmates were being flown to Mombasa to give their statements to the police so they could be used at the trial. He was happy to hear that news, but disappointed that they would not be able to visit him.

Nairobi Bus

The lanky young man stretched and yawned as he stepped down from the overnight bus. Dawn was breaking giving a rosy glow to the eastern sky. It was brisk. A cool morning breeze blew scraps of paper around the bus park. He looked around, pleased with the upcountry temperature, a far cry he concluded from the infernal heat of Mombasa. The bus park was already crowded with hundreds of folks beginning their day by disembarking from dozens of matatus, Nairobi's ubiquitous collective taxis. A young vendor sidled up with a pan of hard boiled eggs for sale. Mayi? He queried. The young man brushed him aside and strode determinedly away. He had an appointment to keep, but knew finding his contact would be time consuming. He decided to walk out Ngong Road to the only address he had. It would give him time to clear his head and go over his report for the umpteenth time.

By mid afternoon, James had been shuttled twice to different locations in the city – first accompanied by a youngster, then driven by a silent older man in a beat up Toyota taxi into the bowels of Mathere Valley, one of Nairobi's sprawling slums. Told to get out of the car in front of a small tea shop, James was met and guided through a labyrinth of alleyways and muddy paths to a mud brick abode, a house indistinguishable from tens of thousands others. It had a very solid wooden door in front and one small window. James was told to enter and wait. His escort hurried away.

As instructed James went in, sat on a stool in the threadbare room and waited. Before long a woman entered from the back room, she nodded and uttered a quiet greeting, locked the door and retreated.

A man coughed, James looked up and a man he knew as George Njorge parted the curtain and eased in.

"James," he smiled, "Karibu, karibu, you are most welcome."

Relieved with the tenor of the greeting, James relaxed. He responded to the welcome, but in Kikuyu. The two men then exchanged a litany of traditional Kikuyu greetings.

"Mary will bring tea," George continued, "but I am anxious to hear your report. I have had no response to my message from other channels. Do you bring any word?"

"It's complicated," James replied with some hesitancy.

"It's okay," George reassured him, "take it from the beginning. Did you find a way to pass my message to the Somali?"

"Yes, I used a cut out like I was instructed, a third party, who could not be identified with us. I choose a Kikuyu girl, a prostitute who uses the same lodging house that I stay in. I gave her the note and the contact phone number. For fifty shillings she was willing to do anything I asked. I supposed that being a whore; she would be able to meet with any man here or there without arousing suspicions."

"So did she pass the message?" Njroge insisted.

"Yes, I am convinced she did. I followed her to the train station about dusk, the hour when the station is most crowded with passengers waiting for the Nairobi train. She spoke to a Somali man and I am sure gave him the envelope. I followed him back to an apartment building, but don't know which one he went into."

"Did you ask her, confirm the delivery with her?"

"That's where it gets complicated." James replied, "You see the woman in question was Monica Njere."

"Ah ha," Njorge sat stunned, "the murdered prostitute." Collecting his thoughts, he probed, "Are we compromised? Have you been identified?"

"No, I think I am in the clear, but the police have taken me as a witness in the case. The inspector believes that Monica was killed by an American sailor. I was caught in the stair well during the investigation and ordered to help solve the case. They took me out to the aircraft carrier – truly a huge ship - to spot the sailor. Later I had to participate in a line up at the police station. Both times I hung back and said little, except it was dark. I was confused and couldn't be sure of anything. I thought about disappearing, but that would point a finger at me – at us – so I'm waiting to be called at the trial."

Njorge mulled it over, "You're correct, it's complicated. I don't give a damn about the dead girl. I hope the American hangs, but I am worried about the special branch. Are you sure there is nothing that could link us – The New Kikuyu Association - to the Somalis?"

"Mr. Njorge," James replied, "I have thought that over a lot. I don't think she knew who we are – who the message was from. I told her it was a confidential letter about a special trade deal. I think she thought I was a smuggler, but she did have the note and the telephone number. I wrote it for her on a slip of paper, but don't know what happened to that. The inspector took everything out of her room."

"So, it's possible that the police have that number?"

"Yes, I guess so."

"I need to think all this over." Njoroge said, "Meanwhile you had best go back to Mombasa and do your duty at the trial. Say nothing more than you have already said. As soon as it is over; come back to Nairobi, we'll find another assignment for you."

A Quandary

After sending James away, Njoroge too slipped out the door and moved cautiously a few twists and turns away to another dilapidated mud brick house, one that he called home for the past few months.

Settling back into a comfortable chair, he mused that it was time to move again. Too long in one place was dangerous. Government spies and informers were everywhere – or at least that is what he had to think.

What about James? Should he be eliminated? He really screwed up: a murder, Americans, police – no end to problems. How deep was he in this Mombasa mess? For the time being, Njoroge concluded, it was best to string him along as he had done. Keep him in the fold, if he passes this test, then review his future.

Meanwhile, the real issue was the Somali. What to do next? Contact would be useful, coordination even better, but the Mombasa number was the only means of getting in touch that he had generated. He'd give Hussein more time to reply, before re-engaging with the Somali shopkeeper in Bilhara Street. If, Njoroge was struck by this thought, if the special branch got the phone number that led to Hussein, then Hussein might well conclude that Njoroge sold him out. A feud with Hussein via the Special Branch would be most unfortunate. Maybe, the New Kikuyu leader thought, I need to pass another message sooner, rather than later.

Departure

Upon exiting the house, James was picked up by the same street urchin, a boy of about twelve, who had escorted him in. "Follow me," he ordered as he wound his way out of the maze of the slum. Upon arrival at a city bus stand on a paved road, the kid asked for a cigarette. James did not smoke, but gave the youngster five shillings, then scrambled aboard a bus headed into the city. He planned to catch the night bus back to the coast.

James thought the encounter with Njoroge had gone well. He had not lied, but had been judicious in revealing only part of events. In truth, he knew Monica because he had paid her for sex on two occasions. The second time, he remembered boasting to her of his importance in a secret pro-Kikuyu organization, saying he was the agent for the coast. He recalled that she had cooed that he was a big man, all the while fondling his privates, but did not know if his bravado had really registered with her or not.

Although he did not flaunt and had not told anyone of these assignations, he feared that somehow this additional connection to Monica would come out in Inspector Oyugi's investigation – may be Monica had told one of the other girls - but so far, nothing. If this twist were revealed, James was sure that he would have more of a case to answer, both to Oyugi and to Njoroge. He renewed his vow of caution.

Testimony

The four seamen arrived a day or so later. With Bonham looking on, da Souza prepped them in his office cautioning them to track the statements they made earlier aboard ship, because the prosecution had copies of those statements. Any discrepancies would be noted. He added that they should not over emphasize their friendship with Tyrell because Kenyan courts tended to discount statements by friends or family. Off they went.

Sworn statement from Thomas Edward Latham. "I, Thomas Edward Latham make the following statement voluntarily to the Kenya Police. I was born on 15 September 1963 in Portsmouth, VA. I am currently assigned aboard the USS America in R-division. On the evening of 5 April 1983 I was with James Mason Tyrell and Earl Ray Whitesides in the Oceanic Hotel bar. After drinking at the bar for about 45 minutes, I assisted Whitesides to our Oceanic Hotel room, no. 216. I left Tyrell at the bar talking with a young black woman. I add that before I left the bar I also talked to the woman and her friend who was named Betty. After I got Whitesides, who passed out, into bed. I started back downstairs, but met Tyrell and the two women coming up the stairs. All four of us then returned to room 216. So, there were five of us there. Whitesides, Tyrell, me and the two girls. It was approximately 1900 at this time. We stayed there until about 2300 when Tyrell and Whitesides left for the ship. I was not in Tyrell's company the entire time since I was in the bathroom for about a half hour from 2100-2130. When I came out Tyrell was still lying naked in bed with the other woman. At this time I would like to describe the hotel room no. 216. It was on the second floor about halfway down the corridor. It had a private bathroom and the main portion of the room contained three beds. I don't have anything further to aid in this investigation."

Sworn statement from Earl Ray Whitesides. "I was born on 2 March 1961 in Springfield, Il. I am currently assigned to the USS America in the R- division. On the night of April 5, 1983 at approximately 1815, James Mason Tyrell, Thomas Edward Latham and I entered the Oceanic Hotel Casino and remained there for about 45 minutes. All three of us entered the hotel bar at approximately 1900. I left about 1930. While there I noticed that Tyrell and Latham were talking to two young black women. I was intoxicated and tired and was helped upstairs to a room rented by Latham, Joseph Clark Davis and Charles Albert Smith. I went to sleep in one of the three beds and did not awaken until about 0100. At that time I noticed that Tyrell, Latham and the two women were in the room. Tyrell and myself left the Oceanic Hotel at approximately 0115 to arrive at fleet landing. We did not have long to wait for a boat that took us back to the USS America. I did not wear a watch so am not sure of the times."

Sworn statement from Joseph Clark Davis." I was born July 29, 1961 in Nashville, TN. I am currently assigned to the USS America in the R-division. On the evening of April 5, 1983 James Mason Tyrell, Earl Ray Whitesides, Thomas Edward Latham, Charles Albert Smith and myself went to the Oceanic Hotel Casino at approximately 1830 and stayed there until approximately 1900. Then we checked out the hotel room, number 216 that Smith had rented. Afterwards Smith and I left the hotel to go downtown. We returned at approximately 2200 to deposit the gifts we had purchased. Tyrell unlocked the door. He was unclothed and walked into the bathroom. I saw Whitesides asleep in one bed and there was a black woman in another. I did not see another woman nor Latham in the room but was told by Tyrell they were on the balcony. Smith and I left the room and went to the bar where we stayed until about midnight. When we returned to the room Tyson and Whitesides were preparing to leave for the ship."

Sworn statement by Charles Albert Smith. "I was born on June 1, 1961 in Minot, ND. I am currently assigned to the USS America in R-division. On the evening of April 5, 1983 I was with James Mason Tyrell, Joseph Clark Davis, Earl Ray Whitesides and Thomas Edward Latham at the Hotel Oceanic bar. Subsequently, we all visited room no. 216 which I rented. Davis and I left the hotel about 2100 to go to town. When we returned about 2200 Tyrell unlocked the door. He was unclothed, but went into the bathroom and came out with pants on. I saw Latham on the patio with a black woman. I exited the room to get some sodas. When I returned Tyrell was fully dressed and had awakened Whitesides. I was in their company until they left for the ship about 2400."

Afterwards, da Souza grilled the four further, seeking leads to any physical evidence that would verify their statements. Smith said he had paid for the room in cash, but did not keep a receipt. Latham confirmed that the name of the girl he slept with was Betty, but did not know more. Davis volunteered that he put through a call to his wife, when they were first in the room that afternoon. He added that the call did not go through then, but because he told the hotel operator he'd be in the bar, the call did come through while he and Smith were at the pool. He spoke from a phone in the lobby.

"Great." Da Souza exclaimed, "This information will be useful."

Bonham reiterated to me that the statements were all the more believable because of the discrepancies of timing. Witnesses rarely remembered things exactly alike. If their stories meshed flawlessly, one ought to be suspicious of a rehearsed concocted alibi. He thought that da Souza would be able to confirm points that would make the alibi hard to refute.

Polygraph

Lt. Commander Bonham introduced me to Special Agent Dennis Wilson, the polygraph expert from Seventh Fleet headquarters in Japan. Randle had earlier asked Inspector Oyugi if he would permit Tyrell to take a lie detector exam. Oyugi said he had no problems with that, but would also check with prosecutor Mbai. He had reported back that Mbai had no problems either, but was checking with the Attorney General's office in Nairobi. On the basis of those assurances, Wilson was dispatched. In the meanwhile, however, things had changed. Tyrell had been charged and was in custody pending trial. Oyugi said he was out of the loop and Mbai stated that the AG's office refused to authorize the test.

Da Souza was indifferent to the idea because, he said," Results of a lie detector test are inadmissible in a Kenyan court." He reported a confidence that Mbai's superiors had rejected the proposal because it risked further inflaming passions to no useful end.

I quizzed Wilson about the validity of an exam. "How can you be sure of the results?

"You can't always" he replied, "but it is very reliable. Let me give you a test and you can judge for yourself."

I agreed and he went to set up his equipment. When he was ready, he wired me up; placing sensors on my chest, arm and finger. He displayed a stack of cards with a number from 1 to 10 on each. He told me to shuffle them then select one and set the others aside. He said beginning at one he would ask me in order if that was the card. I should reply no to every question. First, however, he wanted to check the calibration by asking me to verify my name, address and profession. All questions would only require a yes or no answer, i.e. "Is your name Cliff Nichols?"

I choose number six from the deck and felt that I remained calm and constant throughout the questions. He spoke in a monotone voice. I answered "no" each time. At the end Wilson said that the number was six. He showed me how the jiggle in the lines on the chart revealed my lie. I was impressed.

When examining someone like Tyrell, Wilson said he would ask him the same sort of calibrating questions. Then several inoffensive ones like, "where you in Mombasa on April 5? Do you smoke Marlboro cigarettes?" Then he would hone in, "did you kill Monica Nejere?"

Although I was more convinced of the validity of the polygraph, Kenyan authorities simply would not permit it.

Wilson left a day later to return to Japan.

The Judge

"Good news," I told Hawkins in my regular call to the embassy. "The date for the trial has been set. It will start on June 14. That's only six weeks away. And more good news, da Souza says the judge who has been assigned, C.R. Chesire, is reputed to be honest and fair."

"We'll have to check that out," Hawkins noted. "Chesire, pronounced Ch-si-RE, is a Kalenjin name, so he probably has some back door connections to the power structure. But I hope da Souza's right and that he will stand above the fray."

I went on my weekly visit to Tyrell later that afternoon. Along with a Wilbur Smith novel I took a letter from his mother and asked that Bwana Welfare read through it quickly so I could pass it along. The old man agreed, but perused it carefully. Stamping it "approved" and passing it back he observed that most prisoners didn't get mail. Unless families were nearby and able to visit, prisoners usually lost contact with those outside.

Tyrell's spirits lifted when I gave him the letter. He read it though quickly, tearing up when noting her support and love.

"Jim, I've spoken to your mom and dad a couple of times. I'll stay in touch with them. I've promised regular updates once the trial begins. How's the week been?"

"Terrible as always," he responded, "hot, dull. just waiting." The he added, "But I have had lots of time to think. Getting into this mess wasn't my fault, but it has made me take stock. I haven't really done much with my life. I've just coasted along. I didn't apply myself in school either to studies or to sports. I just sorta hung out. Same in the navy. The work's not much, but I haven't put out much effort. I need to get a focus, decide what I want and then apply myself. After the service, I oughta go to college, if I could get in one."

"Wow," I said, "you have been thinking. Good for you. You need to keep positive and plan ahead."

"Yeah," he replied, "I gotta stay positive, but you, Mr. Nichols, you gotta make sure they don't hang me."

I spluttered, "Jim, now don't think that way. We're doing everything possible to get you out."

On the drive home, I wondered if that was true. Were we doing everything? It seemed so, but the end was not clear. Kenya could hang him and I couldn't promise that it wouldn't.

Watching

After it clanked shut, Jim stood in the door of the remand wing and watched the consul exit across the courtyard through the main gate. There goes my only link, he muttered to himself and I'm stuck here in this hell hole. He again cursed his bad luck in having been fingered for this crime. He bemoaned the fact that he was jailed, charged with murder – a murder that he knew he did not commit. Yet it looked like he might well be convicted. The guys in the jail told him so. No one was ever arrested or imprisoned without being convicted. That's the way the system worked. Once they got you, you were toast. Especially him, they said – he was a mzungu, a white man, never would a white man be imprisoned if he was not clearly guilty. Jim's prison compatriots held out no hope for him, nor for themselves. They were uniformly pessimistic, calmly awaiting their fate – years behind bars.

After a month of incarceration, Jim at least knew the routine. There was not much to it: boring day after boring day. At first the butt of jokes and comments, Jim had steadfastly kept his cool. He had held his ground once or twice, including a brief exchange of blows. But once he showed his mettle, he was more or less accepted.

He had began to sit regularly with a couple of the guys. They were curious about America and asked all sorts of bizarre questions. Evidently their knowledge of the west grew mostly out of Kung Fu movies. However, even as they tried their poor English on him, in turn they taught him basic Swahili. It passed the time.

Often just before dark, in the cooler later afternoon, the remand prisoners played football. Their ball being a collection of plastic sacks wrapped tightly with a few strands of inner tube rubber. Although it usually started slow, the contest could become quite animated. Jim was not a soccer player, but was included anyhow and then became the butt of jibes when he failed to measure up.

In the lazy hours Jim had time to think; to work over in his mind the astonishing array of circumstances that brought him to this point. He blamed the XO for dragging him down to the wardroom where the Kenyan guys pegged him. He had been in town on the night in question, but with his buddies. Even when he was with the girl, two of his buddies were in the room. Others came and went. And she clearly wasn' t the dead girl.

Jim was terribly embarrassed for his parents. Although he had gotten into scrapes in high school, his being arrested for murder of a prostitute in a far foreign land, must be humiliating for them. He could only imagine what the gossips at home were saying. He regretted that he had not established more grown up ties with his folks. He pledged to himself to correct that oversight when he got back home. But just thinking about that brought him back to the reality of his circumstances. Would he leave, or not? It was frustrating not to know, or even worse not to have any control over what might happen.

Business as Usual

I maintained a careful supervisory eye over the Tyrell case even as I went about my other business. There were visa applications to vet, management issues to adjudicate, politicians and other dignitaries to stay in contact with, projects to visit, and more. Yet many of these activities, especially conversations with Kenyans, often led back to the case. Usually, an interlocutor would bring it up out of sympathy to me along the lines of how difficult it must be to keep perspective amidst the negative publicity. I'd ask their views. Most everyone thought that Tyrell was guilty. Otherwise why would he have been arrested? Many Mombasans expressed a fear that once the sailor was hung, the US navy would stop visiting Kenya. I did nothing to disabuse them of that notion. I repeated my personal view that Tyrell was innocent. He was not the man who might have killed Monica. However, folks generally seemed to think that was what I ought to say, so discounted it.

As the trial date approached, Bonham assured me that da Souza was on top of the case. He or his assistant had spent time at the Oceanic checking details. They were also trying to locate Betty, the girl that Latham had sex with, and more importantly her friend, probably named Anna, who was Tyrell's partner.

"Any luck there," I asked.

"No, not that they've told me."

Sometime during this period, Senior Chief Woodley waved a message at me. "Unbelievable," he said, "our man Pope is on the lam again. He snuck out of the brig in Sigonella three days ago and hasn't been found yet. They've asked that I check around to see if he's come back to his girlfriend."

"Didn't he tell you he'd go find her?"

"Yes, but who thought he was serious? I'll head down to Tiwi this afternoon."

Senior Chief found that the overland group, along with Evelyn, had moved on. There was no trace of Pope, then or later. We never knew if he was captured again or not.

The Trial

The morning of June 14th was pleasant, not yet hot. Everything was green as befitting the end of the monsoon rains a month earlier. With the American and consular flags flying, Sebastian dropped Carol and me along with Lt. Commander Bonham who was spiffed out in navy dress whites at the foot of the stair case leading to Mombasa's high court. There was a crowd outside, but we had reserved seating and were ushered in.

The building itself was an imposing one. Built of cut coral stone, it sat at the top of a flight of twenty or so stairs, just up the hill from Fort Jesus. It was undeniably the oldest court building in Kenya, having been constructed by colonial authorities in the 1890s. Stately old mango trees overhung the sides. Inside across a well worn wooden floor that smelt of wax was the court room. The room which sloped downward had seats for about a hundred. A desk for the judge dominated the front with tables for the lawyers and defendant before him. Our seats were on the first row.

Da Souza and Eric his assistant, replete with gowns and wigs were already present, as was prosecutor Mbai. I whispered to Carol that Kenya still adhered to British courtroom attire and courtesies. We agreed that as the day went on they would get hot in such robes. Soon Tyrell was led in. His hands were shackled and he was seated in a prisoner's box to our right. I smiled and mouthed, "Be brave." Da Souza went over, patted him on the shoulder and whispered in his ear.

At precisely 9:00 am, we were ordered to rise. Justice Chesire entered. He too wore a judicial robe and a long white wig cascading down to his shoulders. It looked a little odd at first. His dark eyes and black face peered out from under the wig, but he was clearly quite comfortable. He went right to work. First, he called the assessors by name and told them to come forward. I knew that Kenya did not have trial by jury. Instead up to three assessors were empanelled to hear capital cases along with the judge. At the end he would solicit their view as to guilt or innocence, but would not be bound by it. Of the three called forward, one was a woman of English origin, another an Asian man and the last a black Kenyan. All three were, of course, Kenyan citizens. I recognized the woman. She was a middle aged teacher at one of the private schools in town, married to a Swahili man. The Asian said he was a merchant and the Kenyan professed to be a bank clerk. All three agreed that they were not prejudiced and could hear the case on its merits. I recognized the fact that the three represented the three races of Kenya was not happpenstance, but a deliberate effort to assure balance. They were sworn in.

Judge Chesire told the accused to stand. "You are charged with murder under section 203 of the penal code. How do you plead?"

"Not guilty, my lord," Da Souza interjected.

Looking at Tyrell, Chesire asked, "Is that so?"

"Yes sir, not guilty," Tyrell spoke clearly.

Nodding to the prosecution, the judge said, "You may proceed."

Mbai began, "my lord, the accused James Mason Tyrell is charged with murder. I will show that on the night of April 5, 1983 he strangled Monica Njere to death at the Taita Guest House in Mombasa. Witnesses have identified Tyrell as the perpetrator of this crime. The state seeks the penalty proscribed for murder, death by hanging."

And so it began.

Mbai called James Ndaka, the room rent collector who found Monica Njere's body. He said he was making his rounds in the Ttaita Guest House on the morning of April 6 about nine o'clock. He knocked on Monica's door, but there was no response. He knocked again; still nothing. Then he tested the handle, it unlatched so he pushed the door open, said hodi hodi, then saw the woman lying on the bed under a cover. Froth was coming out of her mouth. She was not breathing. He realized something bad had happened, so left hurriedly, closed the door and reported to the nearby police station. Asked if he had touched anything in the room, Ndapa responded negatively. "Only the door."

Next Mbai called Inspector Pius Oyugi to testify. Oyugi stated that he had been called to the scene after local constables had confirmed the death under suspicious circumstances. One was guarding the closed door when he arrived. "It was a simple room," he said, "with minimal furniture: a bed with metal springs, a table, some clothes scattered around on the floor and some hanging from a peg. The victim, identified by her neighbors, was Monica Njere. She had rented the room earlier in the day and regularly plied her trade from there."

The inspector said he found the position of the body to be odd, not natural. The deceased was lying on the bed, on her back with her legs spread apart and feet fallen through the sides of the springs. She was nude except for a covering. A bloody froth came out of her nose and mouth.

"I could see that she was dead. Given her youth, the position of the body and the matter on her face, I concluded that a murder had probably taken place. There was an empty package of Marlboro cigarettes, a condom package and a used condom under the bed. In addition to clothes, her purse was there. It contained lipstick, a small mirror, her identity card, 112 shillings and a 50 U.S. dollar note. Finding that amount of money there led me to conclude that robbery was not a motive."

"I summoned the forensics team. They collected the items I mentioned and also clipped some of the victim's fingernails for further analysis. They then removed the body to Coast General Hospital morgue for the coroner's inspection. That's standard procedure when the cause of death is in question," he added.

"What did you do next?" Mbai asked.

"I had the constable seal the room and advise the owner that it was not to be entered by anyone. I then began a systematic process of talking to individuals who might shed light on what happened."

"Did you find any?"

"Yes, three men and two women stepped forward to relate that the victim, who was in the sex trade had brought a client to the hotel the evening before. He was a white man and judging from his dress, behavior and a lighter from the USS America, they believed him to be an American sailor. They all got a good look at him."

Da Souza interrupted, "objection, my lord, the inspector cannot provide testimony for witnesses, they must do that themselves."

"Correct," the judge ruled, "objection sustained."

"Yes, my lord," Mbai concurred. "Inspector, thank you for your testimony. I will call you again to review the investigation, but now I want to call Dr. Mohamed to the stand."

Dr. Mohamed was sworn in. He confirmed that he was the coroner for Coast Province and that he had inspected the body of the deceased on the afternoon of April 7. Looking at his notes, he said, "The deceased was a young African female about 22 years old, medium build. There was a bruise on the left part of her face and temple. Blood and froth issued from her nose and mouth. The tongue was bitten. Eyes were bloodshot. I detected no pressure marks around the neck and no evidence of sexual trauma or bruising to the genitals. My internal examination revealed frothy fluid in the trachea, hemorrhage in the lungs, a bruised left temple and congested brain. I concluded that death was asphyxia due to strangulation. I estimated the time of death to have been plus or minus thirty hours prior to the time of the post mortem examination or about 3:00 am on the morning of April 6."

Mbai queried, "So she was murdered?"

"She certainly suffered physical trauma that contributed to her death."

On cross examination, Da Souza asked, "Doctor, please explain your judgment of strangulation if no indications of that were discovered?"

"Yes," the coroner replied, "the absence of pressure marks is not inconsistent with strangulation. The internal evidence was conclusive that she died from violent asphyxia, the inability to breathe."

"Thank you. And could you please explain your estimate of the time of death which you put at about 3:00 am. How much variance could there be in that time?"

"The time of death is a reliable estimate, but allowing for error of two hours, the death could have occurred as early at 1:00 am or as late as 5:00."

"Finally, Doctor, did you detect the existence of sexually transmitted disease in the deceased?"

"No, no swelling or inflammation was readily observable, but I did not perform additional tests for STDs."

"Thank you, Doctor." Turning towards the judge, he advised, "no further questions, my lord."

Prosecutor Mbai advised that he would now call witnesses who had been present in or around the Taita Guest House on the night in question. First was Maria Kyalo.

"Tell us what you saw on the evening of April 5," Mbai instructed.

"I have a room on the second floor of the house at the end of the hallway. On that night I was in my room with my boy friend. We had sex. He was sleeping and I was half watching t.v. and dozing off. I was awakened by a woman's scream. It sounded like it came from outside. I got out of bed and went to the window and looked out, but saw nothing and heard nothing more. This was about ten o'clock because the show was just going off. Later I got up again and went to the choo (toilet) down the hall. I passed by Monica's room and saw that the door was open. I thought someone had just stepped out, but coming back from the toilet, it was still open so I peeked in. It was dark, but Monica was lying nude on the bed apparently asleep. I did not go check on her, but closed the door. In the morning James knocked on my door to tell me that my neighbor was dead. Florence and I looked into the room, but did not go in. James went for the police."

"Did you see anyone with Monica?"

"No," Maria answered. "I knew what she did for a living, but I did not see her with anyone. I heard from Florence that she had brought a white man to her room that night. But she was the only one there when I closed the door about midnight."

Next on the stand was Florence Gitonga. She said that she too was a resident at the Taita Guest House and had been there on the night in question. She said, "About ten o'clock, I left my room to go to the toilet. I saw a white man in the hallway. He seemed nervous. He put his hand to his face and hurried down the stairs. He was wearing jeans and a white shirt. I did not see him very clearly then because the light was bad, but I recognized him later when the inspector brought him to the house."

"Did you hear a scream?" Mbai asked.

"No," she replied, "I did not."

Da Souza rose to ask, "Can you say from which room this white man came?"

"No," she replied.

"Then he could have come out of any room on that floor or the one above?" He probed.

"I guess," she answered.

Da Souza pressed on another point. "Did you participate in the identity parade on board the ship or the line-up at the police station?"

"I did not go to the ship because I was afraid, but I did go to the police lineup."

"Did you pick out the man you saw at the guest house that night?"

"I was confused."

"Did you pick him?"

"No, it was someone else."

Addressing the bench da Souza noted, "My lord, let the record show that Florence did not identify James Tyrell as the man she purportedly saw that night in the police line-up, even though the police had irregularly displayed him to her just the day before."

"Point noted, "Chesire stated.

Mbai next called Salim Said, the taxi driver. Salim stated that he knew Monica and regularly drove her and her clients to and from the guest house. He confirmed that he stationed his vehicle, a white Peugot 404, on Station Road, around the corner from the guest house. He picked up fares from the neighborhood throughout the afternoon and evening and generally worked until after midnight. When not driving he sat and chatted with watchmen or men who might be hanging around.

On the night of April 5, Salim swore, "About ten thirty, a white man came out of the Taita Guest House entrance. He said he wanted to go back to his ship. I agreed and off we went. He told me that he did not have much money, only ten shillings, but he gave me a cigarette lighter with the USS America crest on it. I agreed and took him down Kilindini Avenue to the port entrance, but he said that was not the place. I decided then that he needed to go to Mbaraki pier, but that was too far away, so I dropped him at the Castle Hotel where he could get on a U.S.navy bus."

"How did he seem? What was he wearing?" Mbai asked.

"He was not a big man, about five feet five or six inches tall. He had light brown hair, cut close like a soldier. He wore jeans with a yellow stripped shirt. He seemed to be in a hurry, but did not talk."

"You got a good look at him?"

"Yes, I did."

On cross examination Da Souza asked, "Did you go out to the aircraft carrier?"

"Yes, I did. It was a huge place."

"What happened there?"

"The three of us who went sat separately and looked at hundreds of men who walked by. I did not see the man that gave me the lighter. Later while we were waiting to go back to shore, two other men were brought before us. I said that one of them looked like the man I remembered."

"My lord," the defense lawyer said, "we must be clear on what transpired aboard the carrier. When indicating the suspect the witness said in Swahili "ni kama yeye" that translates as you know to "like him." My lord, that is not a definitive identification."

At the conclusion of this testimony, the proceedings closed for the day. I asked Bonham, who had taken a book full of notes, what he thought. "Good, so far. Da Souza handles himself well, the judge seems open to the evidence."

"What about the discrepancy in the time of death?" I asked, "Is that important?"

"Not really," Bonham replied, "If a violent action causes death, that's murder, even if death occurs later on. But it is possible grounds for a lesser finding than capital murder."

Fulfilling my consular responsibilities I went to see Tyrell in the court's holding cell. We both expressed relief that the trial was finally underway. I assured him that I would call his parents within the hour to update them on what was happening. I told him that he was looking good and bearing up well as befitting a U.S. navy sailor. He smiled grimly, but then had to go, placed in irons, to the van waiting to take him back to prison.

Reflections

Justice Chesire retired to his judicial chambers. He quickly doffed his wig and gown and felt the relief of a cool breeze caressing away his sweat. He always hated trying cases in Mombasa, the heat was just too much. He himself was from the high plateau near Eldoret far to the west where the air was clear and cool. An outstanding student he took his university and law degrees at Oxford. Back in Kenya now for fifteen years he had risen to prominence in the judiciary. He was worldly enough to know that his Kalenjin background was an endorsement of loyalty in the Moi era, but he firmly believed that he had not played that card during his career. He took pride in being deliberate and very careful to rule on points of law.

He knew, however, that he had been chosen to handle this hot potato case. Even so, he had been assigned as if it were normal procedure. He had heard intimations from colleagues that he would be expected to do the "right thing," but the gossips had studiously avoided stating whether that would be guilt or innocence. Chesire had mulled over how the "wrong" verdict might affect his career, but concluded that he would forge ahead in his usual manner. The chips would fall as they may afterwards.

Chesire thought that the day had gone well. He was concerned with all the hoopla – the press and the crowd - outside the courtroom, but convinced that order had prevailed within. He renewed his determination to keep the circus outside.

Identification

In the morning the papers led off with reports of the trial, but they were less provocative than previously. They reported straightforwardly the testimony of those who found the girl and the conclusions of the coroner. That was certainly enough to sell papers.

We assembled as before in the court room. Tyrell was led in and placed in the accused's box. Chersire was punctual. The proceedings started on time.

Mbai continued with witnesses from outside the guest house, starting with Samuel, the night watchman. Samuel said he was sitting on his bench, on the street side outside the guest house entrance. He confirmed that he guarded the housewares store as well as the guest house, plus the neighboring building. "I remember seeing a white man come out of the guest house doorway about eleven p.m. He walked over to Salim's taxi, so Salim went quickly. He got in the car and they left. I recall that he was slim, about medium height, with sandy hair. He wore blue pants and had a yellow stripped shirt. He seemed agitated, in a hurry to get away."

"Did you see this man again on the carrier?"

"I saw three men there who looked like him, but was told that two of them had not been in town that night. That is the third one there." He pointed at Tyrell. The audience gasped.

"Silence!" Chesire ordered. The court room settled down. "Questions, Mr. da Souza?"

"Thank you, my lord," I just want to be clear on identification. "Now, Samuel, you said that you picked out three men while on the carrier that resembled the man you saw that night is that correct?"

"Yes," he responded.

Da Souza continued, "and one of them was the accused? He was, wasn't he, selected by you and Salim at the end of the formal identity parade because you felt that you must choose someone before leaving the ship?"

"Objection, my lord" Mbai interjected, "he's badgering the witness."

"Sustained, move along Mr. Da Souza."

"Yes, my lord, Samuel, did you participate in the police identity parade on April 10 at the Central Police Station and did you pick out the accused at that time?"

Samuel hesitated, "I was there that day. All of the wazungu looked alike. I could not choose."

"So you did not identify him that day as the man you saw on the night of April 5 outside the Taita Guest house." Samuel nodded. "My lord, let the record show that the witness did not identify the accused as the man at the Taita Guest House on the night in question."

Finally, Mbai called James Githiri to testify. Githiri confirmed his name. He said he rented a room at Taita Guest House on the third floor.

"Tell us what you saw on April 5." Mbai counseled.

"Well, I had been out. It was between 10:30 and 11:00 at night. I greeted Samuel and Salim outside, but when I was climbing the stairs. A young white navy passed me coming quickly down the stairs. He did not speak and I don't remember if I did."

"Can you describe him?"

"He was a small man, with light hair and a mustache. He wore jeans and a white shirt. He looked like one of those visiting sailors, so I assumed that is what he was."

"Did you later see him again – on the ship or at the police lineup?" Mbai asked.

"I could not be positive," James concluded.

Da Souza did not bother to cross examine the witness. Mbai then moved on to the physical evidence. The police chemist took the stand. He reported that he had examined evidence from the crime scene: a Marlboro cigarette package, two cigarette butts, an empty Durex condom package, and a used condom. He noted that he had a blood sample from the deceased as well as clippings from her nails.

"What does this evidence show?" Mbai inquired.

The chemist responded, "Both the cigarette and the condom package were not of the type available in Kenya. Thus, I conclude they were brought in from elsewhere. This buttresses the conclusion that whoever was in the room with the deceased was a foreigner. Furthermore, I was able to define the blood type of the man that provided the semen. His blood was type O. I was not able to determine whether it was negative or positive. The deceased was also blood type O and again I could not determine further. Inspection of the nail clippings did not reveal any foreign matter."

Mbai pressed on, "Did you also test blood from the accused?"

"Yes," the chemist replied, "I did. His blood is type O as well."

Upon cross examination, Da Souza thanked the chemist for his effort, but said he had only one question. "What is the percentage of the population that has type O blood?"

"It is generally accepted that well over half of the population has type O blood."

"So, what is the significance of this finding."

The chemist advised, "the fact that the donor of the semen and the accused both have type O blood rules the accused in as a suspect rather than excludes him."

The chemist was dismissed. The prosecutor announced that he would recall Inspector Oyugi to the stand.

"Inspector," he began," after you had learned that a white man, probably a sailor from the USS America, had been in the room with the deceased, how did you proceed?"

Oyugi scowled a minute before replying, "Well, there was a murdered girl and we needed to find the perpetrator. I had four witnesses. I explained the problem to the U.S. Navy man, his name was Randle, who was here to liaise, that's the word they use, with the Kenyan police during the ship visit. He told me that over a thousand men had been ashore that night and that most would be back on their ship. He suggested that we take the eyewitnesses out to the ship and have them look at the sailors there. It was my only option so I agreed. I along with three witnesses, two fellow inspectors and an interpreter sent by the U.S. Consul went to the ship the next morning. During the identity walk pass, the witnesses identified several suspects, but settled on one, the accused in this case James Mason Tyrell."

"Tyrell," he continued, "had been ashore on the night in question. He had been to the Castle Hotel where he met the deceased in the afternoon. Although he went off with his friends to the Oceanic Hotel, he returned to the Castle about 9 to see Monica Njere. They went to her room, had sex, perhaps an argument, and he strangled her. He then departed by taxi, paid with the USS American lighter and was dropped at the Castle. From there he returned to the Oceanic, met his friends and returned to the ship."

"How can you be sure that Tyrell was the murderer?" Mbai asked.

"Four witnesses saw him and placed him at the scene. He fits the description of the murder. His blood matches as the chemist noted. He smokes Marlboro cigarettes, but claims to have lost his lighter. Logically it was the one handed over to the taxi driver. Finally, even though he and his friends concocted an elaborate story about their time in Mombasa. It does not exclude the fact that unbeknownst to them, he snuck away and murdered Monica Njere."

Oyugi elaborated, "according to his own admission Tyrell was present in the Oceanic Hotel in the early evening hours of April 5. But when he and others said they went to a hotel room about nine, Tyrell in fact hurried over to the Castle Hotel for his pre-arranged meeting. The crime then transpired as described. Afterwards Tyrell found himself back at the Castle and managed to reach the Oceanic by 11:30 or so when the group returned to Mbaraki pier."

Prosecutor Mbai sat. Defense attorney da Souza rose. "Inspector," he began, "thank you for your work on this case. You have shown without doubt that Monica Njere died, probably as the consequence of a struggle on the night of April 5. I appreciate your inquiry into this death. Before I begin to elaborate on the accused's whereabouts on the night in question I would like to ask you a few questions."

Oyugi nodded assent, Da Souza continued, "you were obviously at a disadvantage in identifying a suspect who was in the U.S. Navy and probably aboard a ship out of Kenya's reach. How did you find the cooperation from the Americans? Could you ever have identified a suspect without their help?"

Oyugi visibly tensed a bit, "They helped," he admitted, "but they have their procedures and we Kenyans have ours. After Tyrell was presented as a suspect, it took several days before he ended up in Kenyan custody."

"But to clarify Inspector, without American cooperation, you would never have identified or charged this man with the crime. Isn't that so?"

"Yes," Oyugi conceded.

"My lord," Da Souza turned to Justice Chesire, "may I suggest that we adjourn for the day and begin defense arguments tomorrow?"

"Excellent suggestion, we will reconvene at precisely nine in the morning." Chesrie tapped his gavel.

High Considerations

Glasses clinked lightly as the steward added a tot of water to the 10 year old single malt whiskey. Cheruiyot swirled his around savoring the aroma before taking a sip. He mused to himself that a stiff afternoon libation was perhaps the best legacy of the colonial era.

Other ministers soon joined him in the State House library.

"Gentlemen," Cheruiyot began," I have just gotten off the phone from my man in Mombasa. Today's events at the trial were not especially inflammatory. Frankly, Amos your prosecutor did not put forth a compelling case."

"Agreed," the Attorney General nodded, "He had to work with what he had. But it's still a valid accusation. Don't forget the dead girl and the evidence that links the sailor to her. However, we have not yet heard the defense."

"Indeed," Cheruiyot chuckled, "My man said that the Asian lawyer is strutting around like a peacock looking for a hen, jumping on every little discrepancy. My confidant said the court room was a circus. The room is packed as is the press gallery. The U.S consul sits on the front row and beside him a U.S. navy officer in the whitest of white uniforms. Elsewhere in the chamber are the victim's mother and aunts. I was told," he confided with a sly smile, "that an anonymous benefactor financed their trip to the coast. This time there will be no American mother crying for her wayward son, but a Kenyan mother crying for her murdered child."

"What's next?" the Foreign Minister queried, "how will justice run its course? I must remind you all that Kenya is under an international microscope with regard to this case. It must proceed on its merits."

"Yes, Robert," Cheruiyot calmed him, "you've made that point before and a good one it is. The two elements to weigh are first the domestic reaction to the trial and secondly the international one, specifically the Americans. My inclination at this time is to stay hands off. Let it play out. The government is already seen to be concerned for this poor girl. As for the Americans let 'em stew. That's enough for the moment."

Stewing

I returned to the office in the late afternoon and made my reporting call to superiors in Nairobi. I recounted the day's proceeding noting that the prosecution had not put anything more incriminating on the table. Since they had closed their argumentation, they probably judged they had enough. "It seems to be thin gruel," I concluded. "What is your reading of the government?" I asked, "Are they going to make an end run on us?"

"So far," the ambassador advised, "although I understand high ranking officials are watching carefully, the posture seems to be hands-off. That, of course, could change, but the foreign minister has gone out of his way to assure me that the trial will be fair. I have to accept such assurances at face value."

"Good," I conceded, "tomorrow da Souza will begin his defense. That should only take a day or so, and then we'll know."

Somewhat reassured by the ambassador's perspective, I telephoned Tyrell's parents in Pennsylvania. I described to them what happened in court. I reported that Jim was bearing up well and very anxious to have this nightmare finished. Asked about prospects for acquittal, I confirmed my belief that their son had not been involved in this murder. So far, I thought, the prosecution had not made a credible case, but the trial was not over and, of course, I could not promise a favorable outcome. On that inconclusive note, I pledged to call again the next evening.

Before leaving the office, I stuck my head into the visitor's office where Bonham was busily typing at his computer. I admired the guy. Not only did he take reams of notes, but he turned them into an equally long report that same night. I told him not to stay too late and that I would see him in the morning.

Dead End

Special Branch chief Okoth reviewed his options. Virtually nothing had come out of the surveillance and phone tap on the Somali apartment. It seemed to be a complete dead-end. He would have to pull the team off that target. He just could not afford to keep them there in the absence of further leads. Obviously if he had learned nothing from the stakeout, he had nothing to contribute to the murder investigation that Oyugi was running. In any case, Oyugi was already at trial with an American sailor in the docket. Still it was a real puzzle what did the two people have in common? Just a sexual connection or was it more? Okoth did not think that sex was the link. Probably, the whore, who could be visited by anyone, was an unknowing link in a communications system. She had probably been given something to pass on to Hussein and the number to call him. But, Okoth surmised, whatever the connection; she was dead and not talking and the surveillance had yielded nothing. Stymied, it was time to move on.

On second thought maybe he was looking the wrong way. If there was a communication to the Somali, who was it from? Okoth doubted if a Somali Islamist network would use a cut out like the girl in their system. Somalis would stick more to their own kind. As best as he could determine they used safe houses, clandestine meetings and young Somali men to pass oral messages at mosques, and the like. Both Somali tribal identity and Islam provided cover. Hussein's security was very good. That's why he was so hard to find. Then who? Okoth mulled it over. The only possibilities that made sense were internal and the best bet would be Kikuyu dissidents, perhaps the shadowy group calling itself the New Kikuyu Association.

Okoth knew, however, that even just suggesting this possibility would raise red flags all around his headquarters. Tribalism was the great discordant in Kenya and making the charge that Kikuyu dissidents were linking up with Somali terrorists would stir the pot. The Kalenjin power structure would react defensively and some of the harmony established even within the Special Branch itself would be compromised. Okoth did not want to instigate that with a wild speculation. Yet, his duty was to protect the state from subversion and obviously both those groups were subversive.

He mulled over his options. Finally, he decided he would advise headquarters that the Somali side of his investigation, i.e. from the prostitute to Bile, if that's what it was, had gone cold. Consequently he was trying to figure out who might have been sending something via the girl. He would suggest that another internal group might have instigated the contact and he would solicit Nairobi's views on who that might be.

The Defense

The morning was bright and warm. A sea breeze stirred the trees and promised some relief from the heat. The morning paper featured an interview with Monica's mother. She came across as befuddled by the legal proceedings, but confident that the slayer of her child would be convicted. She described Monica as a good girl, 'Always attentive to her elders and a hard worker.' Mom lamented that a lack of school fees had impeded Monica from getting an education, but noted that she had come to Mombasa for "better prospects." The piece was obviously a successful attempt to keep the focus on the trial and the victimization of the dead girl. Well done, I thought, it will keep selling papers. However, the report from yesterday's proceedings was straightforward.

Even a quick reading tended to indicate that the prosecution had little evidence. Yet, the presumption was that Tyrell was guilty – or else why would he be on trial?

We took our respective places in the courtroom. Jim looked worn and apprehensive whereas da Souza was almost bubbling over with his chance to take center stage. When all was ready, he began.

"My lord, today I will present a defense against the charges leveled at the accused James Tyrell. We have heard the prosecution's case to the effect that Monica Njere was found dead, apparently murdered on the night of April 5. The prosecution also effectively linked that crime to a white man, probably a sailor from the USS America. I will not contest those findings. I will, however, prove to the court that the perpetrator of the crime was not, I repeat, not the accused James Tyrell. The defense consists of two parts, first identification and second alibi.

"Identification is key. Let us look carefully at the two times James Tyrell was supposedly identified as involved. The first instance was on board the USS America, following an identity parade on board ship. I would note, my lord, for the record that the so called identity parade while a laudable effort on the part of U.S. Navy authorities to help in the investigation, did not, I repeat, did not meet even the most minimal standards for such a proceeding under Kenyan law. Even so, my lord, the three witnesses taken to the ship that day signaled out several persons as possible suspects. All those were exonerated on account of the fact that they were not on shore on the night in question. Finally, as the witnesses and their escorts were waiting to depart two other men, including the accused, were brought before them. It was their last chance to finger someone. One witness, Salim Said, said that James Tyrell, and I will quote his words as spoken in Swahili, "ni kama yeye." That, of course, translates as "is like him." Not "that is him." Thus, the initial selection of James Tyrell as a possible suspect was only an indication that Tyrell resembled, I repeat resembled, the man Salim saw at the Taita Guest House. Not that Tyrell was that man.

The second identity parade took place at the Central Police Station on April 10. This undertaking did conform to Kenyan practice. At the request of police authorities , the U.S. navy provided six white men of the approximate age and appearance of the accused to participate in the event. The three original witnesses from the Taita Guest House, plus a fourth, Florence Gibonga, who also claimed to have seen a suspect in the hallway on the night of the murder, were asked to identify that suspect. Of the four eyewitnesses, three were unable to make any selection and the fourth chose one of the participating sailors, a man who had not been in Mombasa on the date in question. None of the witnesses identified the accused James Mason Tyrell as being the man they saw on the night of the crime.

"My lord, based on these facts, we must conclude that no effective identification of the accused James Mason Tyrell was made. Instead, because he was named on the ship and was ashore on the night in question, he was unfortunately the only sailor available to the Kenyan authorities to be charged with the crime. And so he was. My lord, there is no identification and no credible evidence tying this man to the victim or to the crime.

"My lord, the second point of defense is that of alibi. I know, my lord, that you understand what alibi is, but let me restate it so all in the courtroom may know."

"You may proceed," the judge nodded.

"Alibi simply means that the person in question was somewhere else doing something different than that alleged by the prosecution. I will demonstrate to the court that the statement given to the police by James Tyrell concerning his activities on the day in question is accurate. As the court knows Tyrell's statement was corroborated by several other sailors who were also ashore at the same time. Although the statements stand valid on their own, additional evidence I will introduce proves them to be accurate. The court will note that all of the statements were introduced as evidence in the committal bundle of documents for this proceeding. In addition to the statements provided by the prosecution, I would like to introduce into evidence the statements the five men made to the U.S. Naval Investigative Service personnel aboard the USS America on April 7."

Mbai jumped to his feet. "Objection. My lord, statements made by U.S. Navy personnel to U.S. Navy personnel are not relevant. And as my colleague has noted their statements to Kenyan authorities are already in evidence."

"Mr. Da Souza?" Chesire queried, "what say you?"

"Thank you, my lord. First of all, the statements are relevant as they link directly to the statements the men made to the Kenyan police on April 10. That linkage already exists. However, I ask that they be entered precisely because they clearly show that the alibi defense I will present is not, I repeat not, a concocted story, but the truth as remembered by five individuals who were formally interviewed separately by legal authorities within minutes of James Tyrell being pinpointed as a suspect. If permitted, the court will note that the two sets of statements are nearly the same, thus also refuting as well any allegation that the various statements were coordinated after the fact."

"Objection overruled. The statements given on board the ship are accepted. You may proceed."

"Thank you, my lord. First, however, let me review elements from the statement that James Tyrell gave to the Kenya police on April 9. This was his account of his day in Mombasa on April 5.

"Tyrell and companions came ashore in the afternoon. They landed at Mbaraki wharf, then took the U.S. Navy leased shuttle bus that stopped first at the Castle Hotel and then at the Mission to Seamen on Kilindini Road. Tyrell got off there. His description of the mission was accurate. Since he has not been there since, we must assume that he was there that day. This is only the first incidence of his statement proving valid.

"Next we move to the Oceanic Hotel where Tyrell and his companions arrived in mid-afternoon. Tyrell noted that two of his shipmates, Smith and Davis, rented a room, number 216. Both these men in their statements said the same thing. My lord, I would now like to enter into evidence the ledger from the hotel for the date of April 5. It shows that Mr. Charles Smith paid cash for room 216. It also indicates that he asked for a room with three beds. The notation on the ledger in the handwriting of the clerk on duty that day, Mr. Ali Wazima, indicates that room 216 had an extra bed in it that day. Furthermore, I would introduce into evidence copies of the phone records from the hotel for that day. Seaman Davis placed a phone call to the United States to his wife. Although he placed the call from room 216, it did not go through for an hour or so. The records indicate that Davis took the call from the telephone in the lobby.

"My lord, the sum of these records from the hotel is to verify the statements made to sustain the alibi. The records definitively show that the group Tyrell was with, rented room 216 as they stated and that Davis called his wife in the U.S. as they all also alleged.

"But, there is more. My lord, all visitors to the casino at the Oceanic Hotel are required to sign in upon arrival. I would now introduce into evidence the registration book for the casino. It shows halfway down page 17 that Jim Tyrell, address USS America, signed in at 6:45 pm. Tom Latham signed in on the next line. My lord, this evidence corroborates the statements of the two men that they entered the casino shortly before seven pm on April 6. It is proof that Tyrell was at the Oceanic as he swore on the day in question.

"Let me turn now to the girls that Tyrell and Latham entertained that evening at the hotel. Their names were Anna, reportedly from Nairobi and her cousin Betty, perhaps from Likoni. My investigator was not able to locate these women, but given the fact that many such persons flock to Mombasa when U.S. Navy ships visit, that is not too surprising. However, a key element of the alibi story related to them is verifiable. My lord, the court will recall that Tyrell stated that he had proceeded up the stairs to the room but looked back and found that hotel personnel had stopped the women. He then went back down and confirmed that they were his guests. Then they were permitted to go upstairs. Mr. Wazima from the Oceanic Hotel confirmed the hotel policy of not permitting unescorted, unregistered guests to leave the public areas of the hotel. Again, my lord, because the detail of this procedure, which would be unknown to anyone unless they had experienced it, reinforces the credibility of Tyrell's statement.

"Now we come to the crucial hours between nine and eleven pm when the murder was apparently occurring on the other side of town. Where was Tyrell? He was in room 216 of the Oceanic Hotel. He engaged in sexual relations with Betty. Also in the room or on the balcony of the room were Latham and his date Betty. Earl Whitesides was passed out in one of the beds. Not only do the two sailors provide substantiating detail of those hours, but the other men who came in and out of the room later in the evening also verified that Tyrell was there.

"There is one more point I would raise in regards to the sexual encounter between Tyrell and Anna. Tyrell said that he did not have one so did not use a condom. It was an error he later regretted as he was treated for gonorrhea on board the ship on April 7. I would like to enter into evidence a statement from the medical officer on the USS America to that effect. My lord, I point this out because of the prosecution's charge that the perpetrator of the murder did use a condom. If as the prosecution concedes that Tyrell was at the Oceanic on the evening of April 5, then where is the logic in not using a condom in the first encounter, but doing so in the second?

"My lord, the prosecution alleges that Tyrell left the Oceanic Hotel between nine and ten p.m. in order to meet the victim at the Castle

Hotel. My assistant checked with the taxi drivers that service the Oceanic Hotel. They run a tight operation. Only a certain number of drivers are permitted to take passengers from the hotel. Other taxis may drop guests off, but only those authorized can pick-up passengers. These drivers canvassed among themselves and agreed that no driver had taken a sole white man from the Oceanic to the Castle between the hours of eight and midnight on April 5.

"These same drivers did recall, however, a disagreement with two sailors about eleven o'clock over the fare to Mbaraki wharf. The two exited the taxi they had initially entered and rounding up several more sailors, took another taxi to Mbaraki. Tyrell's statement recounted that incident.

"My lord, before I conclude let me discuss the issue of corroborating statements that is the five statements given by the sailors from the USS America that support the defense of alibi. Without doubt, these statements were made by shipmates of the accused. So it is logical to ask were they concocted, that is were they relating a story that they all agreed to in order to protect their friend. The answer is that there is no fabricated story here. In the first instance the five men involved were immediately sought out and sequestered by U.S. Naval authorities as soon as James Tyrell stated they were ashore with him on April 5. This occurred on the ship, the USS America, on April 7 the day of the so-called identity parade. Sworn statements were taken from the five men at that time. Those statements were made available to the Kenyan police later that same day. But since the statements were not taken by the Kenyan police and thus of questionable utility in a Kenyan legal proceeding, the five men returned to Kenya on April 10 and gave their statements to the Kenyan police. Let it be noted that there are no essential deviations between the statements of April 7 and those of April 10.

"Reading the statements, one notes that there are differences amongst them. One man remembered some details and times, others had slightly differing versions of the same activities. The mere existence of those differences is important. Why? They are important because people do recall times and actions in different fashions. Human memories are diverse. If the five statements had specifics exactly the same, they would be suspect. But these, my lord, are above suspicion. They are honest and true. The collective thrust of the statements accurately describes the activities of the six men, the five shipmates plus James Tyrell, on the day and night of April 5. Additionally, as I have shown in the defense of alibi, there is physical evidence from the Oceanic Hotel, plus other information from hotel personnel and taxi drivers that prove the veracity of the alibi.

"My lord, the sum of these verifications shows that the accused, James Mason Tyrell, was not, I repeat not involved in the murder of Monica Njere. Tyrell was in Mombasa on the night of April 5, but he was at the Oceanic Hotel with his shipmates throughout that evening until he returned to his ship.

"In summary, my lord, in defense of the accused I have, I trust, proved that he was never, I repeat never, positively identified by any of the prosecution's witnesses as the white man that they saw on the night of April 5 at the Taita Guest House. Secondly, I have shown without doubt that the defense of alibi is unshakeable. James Tyrell's whereabouts on April 5 are known and have been confirmed and verified by witnesses and physical evidence. He was not involved in any fashion in the crime for which he is charged.

"My lord, the defense rests."

"Thank you, Mr. da Souza,"

Turning to the three assessors, Judge Chesire told them. "You have heard the case presented by the prosecution as well as the defense mounted on the accused's behalf. We will adjourn today and tomorrow we will hear closing arguments. I ask that you reflect carefully on the matters considered in this courtroom. After we conclude tomorrow, you will have some additional time to weigh the issues, then I will require you to state your conclusion as to the guilt or innocence of the accused."

Alert

Okoth's report to Special Branch headquarters raised many eyebrows. Everyone had been following the murder trial via the papers with great interest. The possible existence of a link from the girl to Somali terrorists coupled with an even more intriguing conspiracy between them and others – everyone immediately concluded Kikuyu dissidents – doubled the stakes. And if, this was an internal Kenyan issue, prosecuting an American was a charade.

The Special Branch Chief who was of course Kalenjin knew he had to alert Cheruiyot, the minister of state responsible for security. He headed for State House where the minister received him without delay.

"What's up?" Cheruiyot asked.

The chief reviewed the information from Mombasa to the effect that a phone number in the murdered girl's notebook led to Bile Hussein. Additionally, the chief related the analysis that as the Somalis were unlikely to use a Kikuyu whore as a messenger, then who might? He concluded that logically it might be other internal dissidents – probably those damned Kikuyu.

The chief concluded carefully that since the trial was nearing conclusion, the minister ought to know that other intriguing information about the dead woman and her contacts was being generated.

"Thanks," the minister stated, "keep developing those leads, but keep them absolutely confidential. There is to be no, I repeat no leaking of this information. Understood?"

Sitting alone, the minister reflected.

Decision Making

"Well, well, well," the minister chuckled. "It has come to this. Amos, your men did not put up much of a case."

"Agreed, but they did the best with what they had. The problem is that they had no legitimate way truly to find the right suspect."

"Correct," the foreign minister interjected, "that's why the case should have been dropped long ago."

"But now," Minister Cheruiyot retorted, "we need to decide. Amos, if we don't interfere what will Chesire rule?"

The Attorney General stroked his head. "It's hard to say, but he is a stickler for the rule of law and under the law, the prosecution's case is not very strong. I suspect he will acquit. Under the circumstances, that would not be a bad result. This case has been closely watched, both here and, as Robert knows, abroad. The facts aside, it has been a well run trial, Chesire is good at that. From a public relations view, an acquittal would burnish our international reputation for fairness and justice. "

"Yet," Cheruiyot mused "the Kenyan public still clamors for revenge for the murdered girl. Additionally, tweaking the Americans will help keep them in their place. "

"I would take issue with both of your observations, Jonah." Robert answered, "the media has reported the trial straightforwardly; the public knows that there is little evidence upon which to base a conviction. As for the Americans, I can assure you that tweaking them with an unfounded conviction will have negative consequences. The fact is that we need America as much, if not more than it needs us. Sure they boss us around a bit and needle us on civil rights and such, but the development assistance they provide, the tourists they send and crucially in this instance, the security they provide, to us and to the region, are important. We should not be prepared to forego those benefits on the back of a trumped up conviction for the sake of a prostitute."

"Now, now, Robert. Don't get too steamed up. I just want to have my cake and eat it too. I think we can do that. The trick is to look sympathetic, which we are, for public consumption on account of the death, but to remain aloof from any indication of meddling in the trial.

Afterwards, we the government – probably you Amos as the Attorney General – will be able to reaffirm the independence, integrity and impartiality of our legal system."

"Yes, Jonah," the Attorney General replied, "that will work. I think that addresses Robert's concerns as well. Sivyo?"

"Ndivyo," the foreign minister concurred. "Jonah, I am pleased you appreciate my points about the Americans. I will spin this carefully to the ambassador. Then, I hope we can put it behind us and move on."

"First," the Attorney General cautioned, "Chesire has to rule. If he convicts, then we'll need a new plan."

Cheruiyot poured himself another whiskey after the others departed. He had earlier decided not to tell them about Special Branch findings of a possible link between the murdered girl and proscribed groups. No need to muddle the pie, he had concluded, when it's only speculation. Additionally, Cheruiyot knew that such information would only further inflame the foreign minister's insistence that the American be acquitted.

Cheruiyot's first and only loyalty was to His Excellency the President. He had in the past and would continue to bend the law, even subvert it, if the President's power or life were threatened. Foremost, however, he was a political manipulator and was able to stack the deck in his favor under almost any circumstance. He did not see Somali agitators as a real threat to the regime, but he viewed Kikuyu conspirators as much more dangerous. Not so much on account of any action they might undertake, but rather because of simmering resentment within the broader Kikuyu community of the administration's Kalenjin orientation. He feared that sentiment could be fanned, especially if authorities over-reacted to tribal provocation. As ruthless as he was, he also was capable of making constrained calls. He relished walking that tightrope.

Minister Cheruiyot's instincts told him that Chesire would acquit. In the aftermath, he would have the Special Branch continue to investigate murder with an eye out for internal elements.

Summations

I picked up Bonham and we went to the court house early. The prison van had been delivering Jim about an hour before trial time. The jailer, who had come to recognize me, let us both into the waiting cell without difficulty. I brought some cookies that Carol had baked. Jim ate them eagerly. He was in good spirits. I passed along his parent's love and best wishes. They too were hoping that this nightmare would soon be over. I asked about conditions at Shemu la Tewa prison. Jim said they had not changed much. Life there was hot and boring, but he was treated fairly.

Bonham said that he thought the trial had gone satisfactorily. "I have observed a number of trials overseas, and this one is going well. The judge knows his business and seems inclined to rule on the facts...and the facts, I think, portend in your favor. Even though he is a bit pompous, da Souza has been careful not to offend. Today, the two lawyers will sum up their arguments. Subsequently, the assessors will be asked for their views. Note that their views are not binding on the judge. His in the only voice that counts. Finally, Justice Chesire will deliver his decision. I doubt if we will get the judge's decision today. Da Souza says that he will normally take a day or two to write it up."

"So," I concluded, "we'll continue to take it one day at a time. Today, closing arguments, and then we wait for the decision."

"Okay," Jim nodded a bit glumly, "I am not going anywhere."

By nine we were all in our seats.

Justice Chesire gaveled the session into order. Nodding to prosecutor Simon Mbai, he stated, "You may begin."

Mbai wasted no time. Pointing at Tyrell, he said, "My lord, there sits a murderer. On the night of April 5 he did with malice aforethought, strangle Monica Njere to death. As I showed during this trial, James Mason Tyrell is responsible for that murder. Why he did it, we do not know, but he was there. Witnesses saw him and evidence substantiates his presence."

I took a moment to study Jim. He sat still, but was obviously tense. His face betrayed no emotion, but I knew he was shaking inside. Being called a murderer in a court of law must be excruciating. Hold on, I found myself soundlessly urging him. Hold on.

Meanwhile, Mbai reviewed some of the evidence especially the now famous lighter bearing the crest of the USS America. Mbai continued, "his alibi notwithstanding, Tyrell did return to the Castle Hotel where he met Monica as previously arranged. He accompanied her to the Taita Guest House where the murder ensued."

The prosecutor paused for dramatic effect. "My lord, the time has now come for the assailant in this crime to be held accountable for his deed. Justice for Monica demands that it be done. Her family requires the closure that conviction will bring. The nation too, Kenyans from all walks of life, needs to see that justice is done. We need to know that visitors to our shores – no matter what important country they come from – are held accountable and responsible for their actions. My lord that burden falls upon this court. The guilty decision to be rendered here will resonate throughout the land providing solace for those who mourn and justice at the end for Monica Njere."

Prosecutor Mbai wiped his brow, gazed carefully around the packed courtroom. Turning slowly towards the bench, he said, "Thank you, my lord, that is all."

A cascade of murmuring spread throughout the court room, but quickly subsided under a withering glare from Justice Chesire.

"Mr. da Souza, you have a summation for the defense?"

"Thank you, my lord," da Souza said as he shuffled his papers. "I would like to begin by thanking you and the assessors for your patience and forbearance during the past days. I would also commend Prosecutor Mbai for his diligence in presenting the case. I would associate myself with his remarks that the purpose of this trial is to deliver justice. The court has heard both the prosecution and the defense. What remains is a fair and just decision.

As you remember, my lord, the defense did not contest the fact of the death of Monica Njere, nor the testimony of witnesses to movements of people in and around the Taita Guest House on the night of April 5. Rather, what we have challenged is the accusation that James Mason Tyrell was involved. In truth, the entire case against him is based on the mistaken assumption that he was involved. My lord, clearly he was not. Tyrell was never, I repeat never, positively identified by any, I repeat any of the witnesses who saw a man in or leaving the Taita Guest House that evening. Nor could any physical evidence link Tyrell to the crime. All the evidence that might be construed to link him to the crime was circumstantial. That is; he is white, an American sailor, was ashore that night, has type O blood and occasionally smokes Marlboro cigarettes. Conceding that all those allegations are correct, one must then ask how many persons fit those criteria. Only the presence of the lighter reduces the number of potential suspects from ten thousand to a thousand or more. But James Tyrell should have been excluded early on. Why?

First, as I noted he was never identified as being at the crime site. Secondly his alibi, his recitation of where he was, with whom and what he did on April 5 is unvarnished truth. He was in Mombasa that day. He was in the company of shipmates. They spent the evening of April 5 at the Oceanic Hotel. Physical evidence from the hotel proves that. Other evidence also corroborates the alibi. Again, as soon as these facts were known, Tyrell should have been excluded as a suspect. But he was not; why not?

The crux of the matter was that the USS America was leaving Mombasa and with it all the possible suspects in the case. Tyrell was the only name available to the Kenyan authorities, so he ended up on trial for his life for a crime he did not commit.

So how do we deliver justice? We must initially ensure that injustice does not occur. We must abide by the rule of law and of evidence. The facts as presented in Tyrell's defense prove that he did not commit this crime. Justice requires that he be acquitted."

"Thank you, my lord." Da Souza sat.

Justice Chesire looked at his watch. "It is now eleven. We will reconvene at three in order to hear the assessors' decisions.

There was a lot of hustle and bustle as the courtroom emptied. Jim was led back to the court room's holding cell in the back. Da Souza came to speak to me and Lt. Commander Bonham. "That's it. Now it is up to the judge. I don't know how the assessors might decide, but their views are only guiding, not binding. Justice Chesire has a history of not paying much attention to them in any case."

I, of course, congratulated da Souza on his summation. He preened with the flattery, but honestly I thought he did a fine job. Bonham too thought da Souza was on track, even though he remained concerned about Mbai's claim that a guilty verdict would send a political message that Kenyans needed to hear. I agreed that was the big unknown. Would the verdict be based on the merits of the case or upon extraneous political factors arising from the court of public opinion?

The court reconvened at three.

Justice Chesire began by addressing the assessors," Lady and gentlemen, you have heard the evidence and the arguments produced during this trial. Now it becomes your responsibility to render a decision. You are not obligated to rule on points of law, that is my job, but rather you have been asked to evaluate the material you have heard and tell me your judgment. The question is whether or not the accused James Mason Tyrell is guilty of the murder of Monica Njere.

Madame, I will start with you. How do you find?"

The lady assessor, English by birth, now a Kenyan citizen and a middle- aged school teacher spoke up clearly. "My lord, Mr. Justice, I believe that the accused is innocent of the charges against him."

The courtroom hummed with tension, but the judge quickly regained control. "Let me caution the galleries that there shall be no outbursts detrimental to the decorum of this proceeding." Turning to the Asian merchant, the judge asked, "Mr. Patel, what is your decision?"

"Sir, I find that the man is guilty of murder."

Again the courtroom hummed, but it soon quieted as all craned to hear the final verdict.

"Mr. Njroge?"

"Your Excellency," the clerk replied, "I cannot decide. I think that both sides made good points. The girl is dead and someone should answer for it, but maybe Tyrell did not do it."

"Mr. Njorge, undecided is not an acceptable answer. What is it that you wish to be recorded?"

"Yes, Excellency. Then... not guilty."

Justice Chesire continued, "I would thank the assessors for their service. At the conclusion of today's session, you are free to go. Your task has finished." Addressing the courtroom, he concluded, "This court will reconvene at nine a.m. on Thursday next for the rendering of a verdict."

A Deal?

So it begins to end, I thought to myself while riding home. I had stopped by the office, phoned Nairobi, phoned Mr. and Mrs. Tyrell and composed a short message regarding the day's events. I knew that Bonham's detailed report – almost blow by blow – would be on its way before midnight. We had a day to wait before the final result was announced. It seemed to me that acquittal was the most likely outcome, but the possibility of political intervention by high authorities to impose a guilty verdict could not be ignored. I looked forward to getting out of the pressure cooker of the trial and back to the more mundane tasks of my regular routine.

While catching up in the office the next morning, da Souza called. "Can I come over?" he asked. "Certainly," I replied, "see you in a few minutes."

I alerted Bonham who met and escorted da Souza to my office. He got right down to brass tacks.

"Mbai came to see me this morning. He is ready to deal and offers ten years for a plea to manslaughter."

Bonham jumped in, "What does that mean? Does he think he will lose or win?"

"He knows he will lose on the merits," da Souza advised, "but he still has the unknown political card to play. He even cautiously alluded to that during our talk. In the end, I think he is bluffing. He's trying to salvage something out of nothing at our expense. However, as Tyrell's lawyer, I have the obligation to tell you and him, and I must be guided by Tyrell's decision."

"So," I stated, "let's go see him."

Off we went. Bwana Welfare was courteous as ever and quickly had Tyrell brought to the visitors room. Da Souza laid out what Mbai had proposed and explained the consequences. da Souza reiterated his belief that Chesire's verdict would exonerate Tyrell. From a legal perspective he could not see grounds for a conviction, but he cautioned that in Kenya not everything was what it appeared and that logic did not often prevail when politics entered the picture. His advice as a defense lawyer would be to reject the plea bargain offer. But to be clear, the consequences of a guilty verdict would be the death penalty.

Tyrell turned to me. I said I agreed with da Souza's views. Additionally, I advised that Ambassador Starke had been in regular contact with top Kenyan officials about the case and had been reassured as recently as this week that a decision would be based on the merits of the case rather than on extraneous factors. I too would recommend that the plea bargain deal be rejected.

Tyrell responded, "I guess I have to do what you think. I couldn't stand being cooped up in this prison for years. That would be a death sentence too."

We reassured Jim that we did not see that outcome. I relayed his parents' love and concern for him and noted my expectation that by tomorrow this time, he would be free.

The last day

Thursday, June 30, dawned hot and clear like most Mombasa mornings. The flowers bloomed and the birds sang. While I breakfasted on the terrace with the boys they chattered away about school and the upcoming summer holiday.

My last day ever in that court room I hoped as I found my seat. The air of expectation was palatable. The press gallery was overflowing and the television cameras camped just outside on the front steps. Justice Chesire was prompt as usual. We awaited his decision.

The judge began:

"The accused, James Mason Tyrell, is charged with the murder, on the night of April 5, 1983, of a woman called Monica Njere at Taita Guest House in Mombasa."

He then began a long summary of the evidence of what transpired that night in the guest house citing names of those involved and summarizing their testimony. The judge recalled the line up aboard the USS America, Tyrell's subsequent arrest, the interrogation of him by the Kenya Police, including a visit to the crime site. During this interrogation Tyrell denied any involvement or knowledge of the crime. Perhaps without being aware of it, Tyrell himself put forward a defense of alibi stating his whereabouts in Mombasa on the day and night in question. The judged noted that the formal defense of alibi had been filed in the court on June 3 and served on the prosecution on that date.

Chesire continued to read his opinion. "The whole case depends entirely on circumstantial evidence and on the correctness of identification of the accused. The identification has been disputed by the defense who says it is mistaken. The case is dependent on circumstantial evidence because though Maria and James said that they each heard a scream, no one gave evidence that it was Monica's scream and no one saw Monica being strangled. When a case is wholly dependent upon circumstantial evidence as is this one, before drawing the inference of the accused's guilt the court must be satisfied that the inculpatory facts are incompatible with innocence and incapable of explanation, upon any other reasonable hypothesis than guilt. The court must decide not whether they are inconsistent with any other rational conclusion, for it is only on this last hypothesis that the court can safely convict. The circumstances must be to produce moral certainty, to the exclusion of every reasonable doubt."

Continuing on with the validity of the circumstantial evidence, Chesire observed that each of the witnesses who saw a white man at the Taita Guest House on the night in question described a different person, one with jeans and a white shirt, one with a yellow striped shirt, one very short, another with hairy arms and another who sported a mustache. He asked rhetorically how many white men had been in the Guest House that night? Obviously, if more than one, then who was with Monica?

Further regarding identification, Justice Chesire cited several precedents wherein the issue of mistaken identification was at issue. Courts had ruled that inter alia "that where the evidence alleged to implicate an accused is entirely of identification that evidence must be absolutely watertight to justify a conviction." He added that even the Kenyan Court of Appeals had held that "no accused ought to be convicted solely on the basis of uncertain identification especially if there is no satisfactory evidence that establishes the validity of that identification."

In reviewing the identity evidence produced by the prosecution, Chesire noted that none of the witnesses had properly identified Tyrell at either of the identity parades or at the crime site. They had only identified the accused as the man they saw from the witness box during the trial itself. Furthermore, the judge cited the Kenya Police regulations governing an identity parade and confirmed that the initial selection of Tyrell aboard the USS America failed in almost every aspect. He hinted that being the case Tyrell should never even have been arrested. Finally, he found the irregular procedure of taking the suspect to the crime site where he could be seen by witnesses prior to an identity parade detrimental to the standard established by law.

Regarding the alibi put forward by the accused, Justice Chesire noted that Tyrell had essentially put forward his alibi during the very first interrogations. He noted the alibi simply could not have been fabricated after the fact. The judged confirmed that it was incumbent upon the Kenya Police to confirm or refute the alibi. He saw little effort towards that objective. Chesire recalled that Inspector Oyugi had accompanied Tyrell to all the relevant places mentioned in the alibi: specifically room 216 in the Oceanic and the casino there. He expressed astonishment that the police did not locate the casino registration book that was so easily found by the defense. Chesire noted that the anecdote about the two girls being prevented from going upstairs in the hotel by the staff until cleared by Tyrell rang true. This practice conformed to hotel policy regarding unescorted women. It "could not have been a made up story." The judge concluded, "All in all the prosecution failed to dislodge the accused's defense of alibi."

Finally, Justice Chesire turned his attention to the witnesses, especially Maria. He said he found her testimony dishonest and her actions, or lack thereof, injurious. For example, she said she heard a scream, but failed to act on it in accordance with the open agreement by all the women at the Guest House to look after each other. Worse, for several days she did not tell anyone else about the scream, even after the death was known. And if as she said in court, she saw Monica lying exactly in the same position she was found dead, then she must have wondered why Monica's legs were trapped in the wire mesh. This should have caused her to find out if Monica were sleeping, drunk or dead. Again, she did nothing.

The judge criticized other witnesses for not acting in response to the crisis, for not coming forward and for concealing evidence from the police. He noted that even the famous lighter was not immediately produced. The judge observed that the demeanor of the Taita Guest House witnesses was that of persons who had no respect for the truth. On the other hand the evidence of persons who supported the alibi, the Oceanic Hotel clerk, the telephone operator, the man who kept the casino register, the assistant manager of the hotel and the group of taxi drivers were all believable.

By this time in the proceedings it was clear where Justice Chesire was going.

He concluded, "After carefully considering and analyzing the evidence advanced by both the prosecution and the defense as a whole. I find that the accused was never with the deceased at any time anywhere in Mombasa on the night of April 5, 1983 and the accused did not visit Taita Guest House on the material night, and, he is not the white man spoken of by Florence, Salim, James and Samuel, if they saw anyone at all, and, I further find that none of the four said prosecution witnesses at any time on the night of 5th April 1983 saw the accused at Taita Guest House. Above all I find that Florence did not identify the accused nor did James or Samuel on the ship, and the purported identification of the accused on the USS America by Salim was mistaken and cannot be relied upon. As a result the identity of the person who murdered Monica at Taita Guest House on April 5 has not been established in this case. I further find that the prosecution has not dislodged the accused's defense of alibi. While not making a specific finding, the evidence in the case suggests the murder of Monica to have been carefully planned and executed by persons who knew her. The story of the white man was used as a cover up for the true murderer of Monica.

For the reasons I have given I, with greatest respect, agree with the opinions expressed by the assessors who found the accused not guilty. I find the accused is not guilty of the charge of murdering Monica Njere on the night of 5th April 1983 and I acquit him and order that he be set at liberty forthwith, unless he is otherwise lawfully withheld."

Delivered and dated this 30th of June, 1983. C.R. Chesire, Judge.

That's how it ended.

The facts

James mastered his nerves and gave his short testimony at the trial. He then caught a night bus to Nairobi. Along the way he played out the scene once more in his mind. That night he had waited hoping to catch Monica in order to ask her about the message, but she had been off whoring coming back twice to the Taita Guest House with white men. He had heard the second one stumbling out near eleven. Thinking it was a good time to talk to Monica, he snuck to the stairs from his third floor room. About half way down his flight, he saw a white man turning to go down the second floor flight. He waited while that man left.

James pushed Monica's door open without knocking. There was no light on in the room, but enough street light filtered through the window so that he could see vaguely and move around easily. Monica was lying on the bed, naked and obviously very drunk. He whispered to her, but there was no response. Looking around James spotted her purse under a pile of clothing. He took it to the window where the light was marginally better. He whirled when she croaked, "Ahya, mwezi." Theft was not his intention, but he wanted no disturbance. Next thing he remembered he was on top of her, grabbing her neck to keep her quiet. She managed a scream and he squeezed harder and harder. Soon she was still. Although breathing hard, he got up carefully and listened. The guest house remained quiet. James hurriedly looked again into the purse, but did not find the scrap of paper he had given her. He shoved the purse under the clothes; made sure the hallway was empty and crept quietly back upstairs.

Afterward

Senior Chief Woodley claimed Jim and took him home so that he could take a hot shower, eat a good meal and call his folks. Since Tyrell did not have a passport, the Navy diverted a supply flight that normally made the run between Italy and Diego Garcia to Mombasa. Within 48 hours, Tyrell was back in Navy hands. I asked Bonham if Tyrell would be sent back to the USS America. He said that was a possibility. In any case, Tyrell would be treated well and probably offered the opportunity for some easy state side training or duty.

Bonham too left as soon as possible. He assured me, and I never doubted him, that he had completed all the paper work for da Souza's fees. I had few doubts that da Souza's fees would soon go up. He relished the publicity, but to his credit, he assessed the situation correctly and played his hand carefully.

The papers headlined the verdict with accurate statements such as "US Sailor Not Guilty!" Their reporting generally tracked the weaknesses of the case that Judge Chesire stressed in his judgment. Some columnists however, lambasted the verdict as a sell out to the U.S., Kenya toadying to American imperialism, or a racially inspired verdict. There was no winning with such commentary, but there were no new developments to hang opinions on, so this soon faded away.

Embassy Nairobi issued a press release welcoming the verdict and expressing the conviction that justice was done. It complimented Kenya for scrupulously observing the rule of law and the rights of the accused. The Kenyan leadership hurried to claim credit for an independent judiciary. Attorney General Makupa was interviewed on a morning talk show on television to that effect. He also regretted that the murderer of Monica Njere had not been found and pledged that the Kenya Police would keep looking. Meanwhile, no heads rolled in

Mombasa, instead the police and prosecution team got a warm atta boy message from Minister Cheruiyot at State House.

Aboard the USS America an un-named sailor breathed easy, relieved with the acquittal. He knew he should have been on trial. He had hooked up with a woman named Monica. They got drunk then went to a seedy room and screwed. She passed out; he left, but remembered giving money and a lighter to a cabbie.

I had a lot of catching up to do. That kept me busy. For several weeks the trial and the result were hot topics among my various contacts, but that soon faded away. The slow steady pace of life in Mombasa reasserted itself. I knew, however, I would cross my fingers, hire a witch doctor, sacrifice a goat and do whatever else it might take to ensure good luck the next time the U.S. Navy came into port.

Epilogue

The New Kikuyu Association faded away as any sort of organized threat, especially after Mwai Kibaki, a Kikuyu, became president several years later.

Hussein apparently went to ground as he planned, but the core of his group was forged by Al Qaeda into an operative arm of Islamic terrorism. It struck some fifteen years later bombing the U.S. embassies in Nairobi and Dar es Salaam.

the end

\###

About the author

Robert E.Gribbin is a retired Foreign Service Officer. In a thirty year career he served in many African nations and from 1981-84 was the U.S. Consul in Mombasa, which is the setting of this novel. Gribbin wrote a well received memoir of his experiences as U.S. Ambassador in Rwanda entitled **In the Aftermath of Genocide - the U.S. Role in Rwanda**. In that book he recounts the rise of the ethnic hatred that led to genocide and the unfolding of the event itself. He dissects the impact of the trauma on Rwanda and its neighbors and the efforts, especially those of the United States, to foster reconstruction, reconciliation and the restoration of peace in the region. Gribbin is also the author of an adventure novel entitled **State of Decay: An Oubangui Chronicle.** Set in a nation that closely resembles the Central African Republic, it is a tale of political intrigue and revolution. Both books are available from on-line bookstores.

Connect with me on line:
http://www.regribbin.com or
http://www.rwandakenya.blogspot.com
A passage from **In the Aftermath of Genocide**

We flew in a United Nations helicopter to the church at Nyarubuye in eastern Rwanda, near the Tanzanian border. Nyarubuye was as far off the beaten track as one could get in Rwanda. Set in a copse of towering eucalyptus trees, the brick church and surrounding buildings sat on the crest of a hill looking out over the lakes and lowlands of the Akagera Park. We landed in a field of high grass just outside the church compound, where we were received by a small delegation composed of the new prefect, the local military commander and a survivor of the genocide. A dozen soldiers stood on discreet guard in a ring several hundred yards around the church. The first thing I noticed was the complete absence of other people. In Africa in general and in Rwanda in particular there are almost always crowds of people, especially at any event that draws a helicopter, but at Nyarubuye there were none. The delegation said that the local population had all fled to neighboring Tanzania two years earlier and had not yet returned.

The wind whistled softly through the trees accentuating the eerie silence. Our guides explained that Nyarubuye had been the scene of vicious killing during the genocide. Tutsi from the surrounding region had sought refuge in the church. They were penned in and imprisoned there for several days until *Interahamwe* squads arrived; after that massacre was methodical. According to the survivor we met, the foyer of the church was set aside as a rape room. He said there was a lot of noise and confusion during the killings, during which he and several others managed to climb over the compound wall and run miles down to the swamps of Akagera.

The church itself was completely empty when we visited, and having been desecrated by the deaths, no longer used. To the side of the church was a courtyard enclosed by a brick wall at one end, and lined by buildings on the other two sides whose doors and windows opened into the courtyard. Obviously, they had served as Sunday school rooms, church offices and the like. However, the rooms were stacked to the ceilings with the mummifying corpses of thousands of human beings.

Near skeletal faces of men, women and children stared blankly. A moldering stench of death hovered in the air. The horror of what had happened there was overwhelming, yet the quiet lent dignity to the repose of the dead.

In respectful tones, our guides explained how the murders occurred. They showed us a large smoothly polished stone in the courtyard worn down by repeated sharpening of machete blades. We saw a bloodstained log where legs had been chopped off., "to make tall ones short" The prefect said that not all bodies had been pushed in to the rooms by the killers. The courtyard and the church itself had been waist deep in death as well. Those bodies had later been moved by RPA soldiers, including the local commander who was present, into the nearby rooms. A crunch underfoot in the knee high grass revealed a human jawbone, which we reverently added to the collection in the nearest room.

And from **State of Decay**

Jeans's chains clanked as he shifted, a noise he hardly recognized any longer. Instead he listened intently for the faint cockcrows and bird calls which floated through the predawn quiet into his cramped cell. It was measure of reality, which he sought daily. Cellmates "Professor" and "Courage" rasped quietly in their slumber. Soon another day in prison would begin - its monotony marked only by the daily rituals and fears of prison life. Jean's mind floated out to the birds, to the freedom of the past. ...

His Supreme Excellency, President of the Oubangui Repblic, Lion of Central Africa, Marc Simplice Bassia stood among the carnage of his bodyguards waving his cane, screaming at the imbeciles to shoot back. One grenade had exploded ten meters away, killing or maiming half a dozen of his entourage. Luckily the portly frame of Ambassador Ouada had absorbed shrapnel meant for Bassia. A second grenade lay at his feet. An old soldier, Bassia saw instinctively that the pin had not been pulled. He railed and ranted, but like the battle -harden sergeant he was, directed his men into action. In the withering fire they laid down, two attackers died along with dozens of traditional dancers and a few airport workers. Bullets whined and ricocheted off the concrete posts supporting the airport's VIP lounge, wounding several more of Bassia's cohorts. As clips were expended, the crackle of gunfire was replaced by the wails of the wounded and screams of the terrified. Bassia retreated unscathed into the sanctuary of the lounge. Ensconced in the cocoon of wide-eyed security thugs, Bassia promised. "The real bloodbath will begin now."